LITTLE WOMEN

A Kaplan Vocabulary-Building Classic for Young Readers

**Look for more
Kaplan Vocabulary-Building Classics
for Young Readers**

Great Expectations
by Charles Dickens

The Adventures of Tom Sawyer
by Mark Twain

Treasure Island
by Robert Louis Stevenson

LITTLE WOMEN

A Kaplan Vocabulary-Building Classic for Young Readers

LOUISA MAY ALCOTT

ABRIDGED

PUBLISHING

New York • Chicago

Published by Kaplan Publishing, a division of Kaplan, Inc.
888 Seventh Ave.
New York, NY 10106

Editorial Director: Jennifer Farthing
Project Editor: Anne Kemper
Content Manager: Patrick Kennedy
Abridgement and Adaptation: Nick Davis for Ivy Gate Books
Interior Design: Ismail Soyugenc for Ivy Gate Books
Cover Design: Mark Weaver

Manufactured in the United States of America
Published simultaneously in Canada

10 9 8 7 6 5 4 3 2

April 2006

ISBN-13: 978-0-7432-6653-6
ISBN-10:   0-7432-6653-6

TABLE OF CONTENTS

HOW TO USE THIS BOOK

Louisa May Alcott's *Little Women* is a classic tale of young women and their journey toward adulthood. It also is a way for today's students to enrich their vocabularies – for tests as well as for daily writing and speaking.

Kaplan makes it as easy as 1-2-3 for you to learn dozens – even hundreds – of new words just by reading this classic story. On the right-hand pages you will find the words of Alcott's famous novel. On each page you will find words that have been bolded (put into heavy, dark type). These are words found on tests you take, both for your school subjects and for standardized tests. On the left-hand pages you'll find information about those words: how to pronounce them, what part of speech they are, what they mean, and even what synonyms they might have. In short, you'll find everything you will need to master each of these special words in the story.

Not all of the challenging or unusual words in *Little Women* are usually found on tests. Some are words that were used most often in Alcott's day, more than 125 years ago. Others are words that are specific to people's occupations or to other things that were common at that time. You might want to learn these words as well, even though they are not likely to appear on tests you might take. For this reason we have underlined them and put information about them in the glossary at the back of this book.

You'll also find other helpful features in this book. One of them is "Louisa May Alcott and *Little Women.*" It provides useful information about Alcott's life and this particular book, all of which will help you enjoy your reading even more.

The back of the book contains a section that will assist you in writing a book report about *Little Women.* Use it as an organizer to develop and order your thoughts and ideas about the book. You will also find discussion questions. These will get you thinking about the characters, events, and meaning of this classic novel. They will also help you get ready to discuss it in class, with friends, or even with your family members.

Now that you have found out what is in the book – and how to use it – you can get started reading and enjoying one of the most famous classics of all time.

LOUISA MAY ALCOTT
AND *LITTLE WOMEN*

Born in 1832, Louisa May Alcott was part of a New England family well known for its progressive values. Although the Alcotts were of "genteel," middle-class stock, they were poor. As a result, much like the March sisters in *Little Women,* the Alcott children took on a variety of jobs.

By the time Louisa was 18, she was a successful professional writer, earning enough to support herself, her parents and sisters, and a number of nieces and nephews. Her true fame came, however, with *Little Women,* a book whose first printing sold out in only a month. A second volume, which continued the tale of the March sisters through adulthood, appeared in 1869 to equal popular response. Since then, *Little Women* has not been out of print. But more important, it has managed to communicate with generation after generation of readers.

Devoted to her family, Alcott struggled to remain alive in order to nurse her dying father until his death in 1888. She died in 1888 just two months after he passed away.

LITTLE WOMEN

DREADFUL (<u>dred</u> fehl) *adj.*
1. causing fear
   Synonym: terrible
2. very bad or unpleasant
   Synonym: awful

CONTENTEDLY (kehn <u>ten</u> tid lee) *adv.*
in a satisfied way
   Synonyms: happily, gladly

CHAPTER 1

"Christmas won't be Christmas without any presents," grumbled Jo, lying on the rug.

"It's so **dreadful** to be poor!" sighed Meg, looking down at her old dress.

"I don't think it's fair for some girls to have plenty of pretty things and other girls to have nothing at all," added little Amy, with an injured sniff.

"We've got Father and Mother and each other," said Beth **contentedly** from her corner.

The four young faces darkened as Jo said sadly, "We haven't got Father, and we shall not have

ALTERED (<u>awl</u> terd) *adj.*
made different
Synonyms: changed, transformed

PROPOSE (preh <u>pohz</u>) *v.* **-ing, -ed**
to put forward an idea or plan
Synonyms: suggest, advise, recommend

DECIDEDLY (deh <u>sy</u> did lee) *adv.*
without doubts
Synonyms: firmly, resolutely

TIRESOME (<u>tie</u> er sum) *adj.*
making one tired or bored
Synonyms: boring, annoying, tedious

him for a long time," reminding them that Father was far away, where the <u>fighting</u> was.

Nobody spoke for a minute. Then Meg said in an **altered** tone, "You know the reason Mother **proposed** not having any presents this Christmas. It is going to be a hard winter for everyone. And she thinks we ought not to spend money for pleasure when our men are suffering so in the army."

"I don't think the little we spend would make any difference. We've each got a dollar, and the army wouldn't be much helped by our giving that. I agree not to expect anything from Mother or you, but I do want to buy something to read. I've wanted it so long," said Jo, who was a <u>bookworm</u>.

"I planned to spend mine on new music," said Beth, with a little sigh, which no one heard.

"I wanted a nice box of drawing pencils. I really need them," said Amy **decidedly**.

"Mother didn't say anything about our money, and she won't wish us to give up everything. Let's each buy what we want and have a little fun. I'm sure we work hard enough to earn it," cried Jo.

"I know I do – teaching those **tiresome**

FRET (freht) *v.* **-ing**, **-ed**
to be disturbed or bothered
Synonyms: worry, brood

IMPERTINENT (im <u>pur</u> tin ehnt) *adj.*
without proper respect or manners
Synonyms: rude, impolite, fresh

PLAGUE (playg) *v.* **-ing**, **-ed**
to bother or trouble
Synonyms: annoy, irritate

LIBEL (<u>lie</u> bell) *v.* **-ing**, **-ed**
to say untrue things
Synonyms: lie, slander

PECK (pek) *v.* **-ing**, **-ed**
to speak sharply or with criticism
Synonyms: insult, criticize

children nearly all day when I'm longing to enjoy myself at home," began Meg, in the complaining tone again.

"You don't have half such a hard time as I do," said Jo. "How would you like to be shut up for hours with a nervous, fussy old lady who keeps you trotting, is never satisfied, and bothers you till you're ready to fly out the window or cry?"

"It's naughty to **fret**, but I do think washing dishes and keeping things tidy is the worst work in the world. It makes me cross, and my hands get so stiff that I can't practice well at all." Beth looked at her rough hands with a sigh.

"I don't believe any of you suffer as I do," cried Amy, "You don't have to go to school with **impertinent** girls who **plague** you if you don't know your lessons and laugh at your dresses and label your father if he isn't rich, and insult you when your nose isn't nice."

"If you mean **libel**, I'd say so, and not talk about labels, as if Papa was a pickle bottle," advised Jo, laughing.

"Don't **peck** at one another. Don't you wish we

SLANG (slang) *n.*
informal language
Synonym: street talk

REPROVING (reh proo ving) *adj.*
not agreeing, finding fault
Synonyms: scolding, criticizing

VAIN (vane) *n.*
overly proud, thinking too highly of oneself
Synonyms: conceited, self-satisfied

had the money Papa lost when we were little, Jo? Dear me! How happy we'd be if we had no worries!" said Meg, who could remember better times.

"You said the other day you thought we were happier than the King children, for they were fighting and fretting all the time in spite of their money."

"So I did, Beth. Well, I think we are. For though we do have to work, we make fun of ourselves. And we are a pretty jolly set, as Jo would say."

"Jo does use such **slang** words!" observed Amy, with a **reproving** look at the long figure stretched on the rug.

As readers like to know how people look, we will take this moment to give them a little sketch of the four sisters who sat knitting away in the twilight, while the December snow fell quietly <u>without</u>, and the fire crackled cheerfully within.

Margaret, the eldest of the four, was sixteen and very pretty, with large eyes, plenty of soft brown hair, a sweet mouth, and white hands, of which she was rather **vain**. Fifteen-year-old Jo was very tall, thin, and reminded one of a <u>colt</u>, for she never seemed to know what to do with her long

TIMID (<u>tim</u> id) *adj.*
easily scared or made to feel unsure of oneself
Synonyms: nervous, fearful, shy

EXPRESSION (ek <u>spresh</u> uhn) *n.*
the look on a person's face
Synonyms: appearance, air

limbs, which were very much in her way. She had a firm mouth and sharp, gray eyes, which appeared to see everything. Her long, thick hair was her beauty, but it was usually bundled into a net in order to be out of her way. Round shoulders had Jo, big hands and feet, a loose look to her clothes, and the uncomfortable appearance of a girl who was rapidly shooting up into a woman and didn't like it.

Elizabeth, or Beth as everyone called her, was a rosy, smooth-haired, bright-eyed girl of thirteen, with a shy manner, a **timid** voice, and a peaceful **expression** which was seldom disturbed. She had never, unfortunately, been in the best of health and suffered over the years from illness. Amy, though the youngest, was a most important person, in her own opinion at least. A regular snow maiden, with blue eyes and yellow hair curling on her shoulders. Pale and slender, she always carried herself like a young lady mindful of her manners. What the characters of the four sisters were we will leave to be found out.

"I'll tell you what we'll do," said Beth. "Let's each get Marmee something for Christmas and not get anything for ourselves."

EXCLAIM (ek <u>sklaym</u>) *v.* **-ing**, **-ed**
to say something strongly and suddenly
Synonyms: assert, shout

SOBERLY (<u>soh</u> bur lee) *adv.*
in a serious and careful way
Synonym: gravely

HEMMED (hemd) *adj.*
folded and sewn
Synonym: edged

COLOGNE (kol <u>own</u>) *n.*
scented liquid
Synonym: perfume

ELEGANTLY (<u>el</u> uh guhnt lee) *adv.*
in a sophisticated way
Synonym: stylishly

"That's like you, dear! What will we get?" **exclaimed** Jo.

Everyone thought **soberly** for a minute. Then Meg announced, "I shall give her a nice pair of gloves."

"Some handkerchiefs, all **hemmed**," said Beth.

"I'll get a little bottle of **cologne**," added Amy.

"And I," announced Jo, "will get her a new pair of slippers."

"How will we give the things?" asked Meg.

"Let Marmee think we are getting things for ourselves. Then we'll surprise her," said Jo, marching up and down, with her hands behind her back and her nose in the air.

"Glad to find you so merry, my girls," said a cheery voice at the door, and the girls turned to welcome a tall, motherly lady with a "can-I-help-you" look about her which was truly delightful. She was not **elegantly** dressed, but she was a noble-looking woman, and the girls thought the gray cloak and unfashionable bonnet covered the most splendid mother in the world.

"Well, dearies, how have you got on today?

PARTICULARLY (par <u>tik</u> yuh lur lee) *adv.*
in an unusual or special way
Synonyms: especially, exceptionally

CHAPLAIN (<u>chap</u> lin) *n.*
a religious leader who works in the military
Synonyms: priest, minister, rabbi

There was so much to do, getting the boxes ready to go tomorrow, that I didn't come home to dinner. Has anyone come to visit, Beth? How is your cold, Meg? Jo, you look tired to death. Come and kiss me, baby."

As they gathered around the table, Mrs. March said, with a **particularly** happy face, "I've got a treat for you after supper."

A quick, bright smile went round like a streak of sunshine. Jo tossed up her napkin, crying, "A letter! A letter! Three cheers for Father!"

"Yes, a nice long letter. He is well, and he thinks he shall get through the cold season better than we feared. He sends all sorts of loving wishes for Christmas and a special message to you girls," said Mrs. March, patting her pocket as if she had a treasure there.

"I think it was so splendid of Father to go into the army as a **chaplain** when he was too old to be drafted and not strong enough for a soldier," said Meg warmly.

"Don't I wish I could go as a drummer or a

QUIVER (<u>kwiv</u> ur) *n.*
a shake or a tremble
Synonyms: shiver, shudder

ENDURE (en <u>dur</u>) *v.* **-ing**, **-ed**
to put up with something difficult
Synonyms: bear, tolerate

nurse, so I could be near him and help him!" exclaimed Jo, with a groan.

"When will he come home, Marmee?" asked Beth, with a little **quiver** in her voice.

"Not for many months, dear, unless he is sick. He will stay and do his work faithfully as long as he can."

True to her word, Mrs. March took out the letter as soon as they had finished their supper. "Now come and hear the letter," she said, and they all drew to the fire.

Very few letters were written in those hard times that were not touching, especially those which fathers sent home. In this one little was said of the hardships **endured**, the dangers faced, or the homesickness conquered. It was a cheerful, hopeful letter. But at the end the writer's heart overflowed with fatherly love and longing for the little girls at home.

Everybody sniffed back a tear when they came to that part, so Mrs. March reminded the girls to be strong, like the characters in one of their favorite books, _Pilgrim's Progress_. Then the table was

ACCOMPANIMENT (uh <u>kum</u> puh nee mint) *n.*
instrument or voice complementing a melody
Synonym: support

PENSIVE (<u>pen</u> siv) *adj.*
serious or deep
Synonyms: thoughtful, meditative,
contemplative

cleared, and out came four little workbaskets, and the needles flew as the girls made sheets for Aunt March. It was uninteresting sewing, but no one grumbled.

At nine they stopped work and sang, as usual, before they went to bed. No one but Beth could get much music out of the old piano, but she had a way of touching the yellow keys and making a pleasant **accompaniment** to the simple songs they sang. Meg had a voice like a flute, and she and her mother led the little choir. Amy chirped like a cricket, and Jo wandered through the notes at her own sweet will, always coming out at the wrong place with a croak that spoiled the most **pensive** tune. They had always done this from the time they could lisp

Crinkle, crinkle, 'ittle 'tar,

and it had become a household custom, for the mother was a born singer. The first sound in the morning was her voice as she went about the house singing like a lark, and the last sound at night was the same cheery sound, for the girls never grew too old for that familiar <u>lullaby</u>.

CRAM (kram) *v.* **-ing**, **-ed**
to squeeze things into small spaces
Synonyms: stuff, force

CRIMSON (<u>krim</u> zuhn) *adj.*
deep red
Synonyms: cherry, rouge

BID (bid) *v.* **-ing**, **bade**
to tell someone to do something
Synonyms: propose, instruct

CHAPTER 2

Jo was the first to wake in the gray dawn of Christmas morning. No stockings hung at the fireplace, and for a moment she felt as much disappointed as she did long ago, when her little sock fell down because it had been **crammed** so full of goodies. Then she slipped her hand under her pillow and drew out a little **crimson**-covered book. It was *Pilgrim's Progress,* the very book Mrs. March had reminded them of last night.

She woke Meg with a "Merry Christmas," and **bade** her see what was under her pillow. A

PRECIOUS (<u>presh</u> uhss) *adj.*
very special or valuable
Synonyms: prized, beloved

RUMMAGE (<u>ruhm</u> ij) *v.* **-ing, -ed**
to search for something messily and carelessly
Synonyms: fumble, delve

green-covered book appeared, with the same picture inside, and a few words written by their mother, which made their one present very **precious** in their eyes. Presently Beth and Amy woke to **rummage** and find their little books also, one gray, the other blue, and all sat looking at and talking about them, while the east grew rosy with the coming day.

"Girls," said Meg seriously, "Mother wants us to read and love and mind these books, and we must begin at once, for I know it will do me good and help me through the day."

"Where is Mother?" asked Meg, as she and Jo ran down to thank her for their gifts.

"Goodness only knows. Some poor creeter came a-beggin', and your ma went straight off to see what was needed," replied Hannah, who had lived with the family since Meg was born, and was considered by them all more as a friend than a servant.

"She will be back soon, I think," said Meg. "Why, where is Amy's bottle of perfume?" she added, as the little bottle did not appear.

NOTION (<u>noh</u> shun) *n.*
an impulsive idea or desire
Synonym: thought

HASTILY (<u>hay</u> stuh lee) *adv.*
quickly and hurriedly
Synonyms: speedily, rapidly

ABASH (a <u>bash</u>) *v.* **-ing**, **-ed**
to make someone feel embarrassed or ashamed
Synonyms: humiliate, humble

"She took it out a minute ago, and went off with it to put a ribbon on it, or some such **notion**," replied Jo, dancing about the room to take the first stiffness off the new slippers she was giving to her mother.

"How nice my handkerchiefs look, don't they? Hannah washed and ironed them for me, and I marked them all myself," said Beth, looking proudly at the somewhat uneven letters which had cost her such labor.

"There's Mother. Hide the basket, quick!" cried Jo, as a door slammed and steps sounded in the hall.

Amy came in **hastily**, and looked rather **abashed** when she saw her sisters all waiting for her.

"Don't laugh at me, Jo! I only meant to change the little bottle for a big one, and I gave all my money to get it, and I'm truly trying not to be selfish any more.

As she spoke, Amy showed the handsome bottle which replaced the cheap one, and looked so earnest and humble that Meg hugged her on the spot, and Jo pronounced her a "<u>trump</u>" while Beth

ORNAMENT (<u>or</u> nuh muhnt) *v.* **-ing**, **-ed**
> to decorate
> > Synonyms: adorn, beautify

STATELY (<u>state</u> lee) *adv.*
> grand and dignified
> > Synonyms: elegant, majestic

HUDDLE (<u>huhd</u> uhl) *v.* **-ing**, **-ed**
> to crowd together in a tight space
> > Synonyms: cluster, group

IMPETUOUSLY (im <u>pet</u> choo uhss lee) *adv.*
> done suddenly and without thought
> > Synonyms: unthinkingly, rashly

ran to the window, and picked her finest rose to **ornament** the **stately** bottle.

Another bang of the street door sent the basket under the sofa, and the girls to the table, eager for breakfast.

"Merry Christmas, Marmee! Many of them! Thank you for our books. We read some, and mean to every day," they all cried in chorus.

"Merry Christmas, little daughters! I'm glad you began at once, and hope you will keep on. But I want to say one word before we sit down. Not far away from here lies a poor woman, Mrs. Hummel, with a little newborn baby. Six children are **huddled** into one bed to keep from freezing, for they have no fire. There is nothing to eat over there. My girls, will you give them your breakfast as a Christmas present?"

They were all unusually hungry, having waited nearly an hour, and for a minute no one spoke. Then Jo exclaimed **impetuously**, "I'm so glad you came before we began!"

"May I go and help carry the things to the poor little children?" asked Beth eagerly.

PROCESSION (pruh <u>sesh</u> uhn) *n.*
a group of people walking together
Synonyms: parade, convoy

ENACT (en <u>akt</u>) *v.* **-ing**, **-ed**
to perform or relate something
Synonyms: embody, execute

ESCORT (<u>ess</u> kort) *n.*
someone who protects others
Synonyms: guide, bodyguard

"I shall take the cream and the muffins," added Amy, giving up the article she most liked.

Meg was already covering the pancakes, and piling the bread into one big plate.

"I thought you'd do it," said Mrs. March, smiling. "When we come back we will have bread and milk for breakfast, and make it up at dinnertime."

They were soon ready, and the **procession** set out. And when they returned, I think there were not in all the city four merrier people than the hungry little girls who gave away their breakfasts and contented themselves with bread and milk on Christmas morning.

Then, when their mother was upstairs, the girls quickly set out the presents. "She's coming! Strike up, Beth!" cried Jo.

Beth played a march, Amy threw open the door, and Meg **enacted escort** with great dignity. Mrs. March was surprised and touched, and she smiled with her eyes full as she examined her presents and read the notes which accompanied them.

The morning charities and ceremonies took so much time that the rest of the day was devoted

GORGEOUS (<u>gor</u> juhss) *adj.*
very attractive and beautiful
Synonyms: dazzling, lovely

TUMULTUOUS (too <u>muhl</u> choo uhss) *adj.*
noisy and unrestrained
Synonyms: disorderly, riotous

SUBSIDE (suhb <u>side</u>) *v.* **-ing**, **-ed**
1. to sink to a lower level
Synonym: lessen
2. to become less active and intense
Synonym: settle

RAPTUROUS (<u>rap</u> chur uhss) *adj.*
showing great emotion or enthusiasm
Synonyms: joyful, elated

to preparations for the evening festivities, which included the performance of a play especially written by the girls. Each year, the girls put their wits to work and made whatever they needed, even pasteboard guitars, **gorgeous** robes of old cotton glittering with pieces of tin from a pickle jar, and armor made of metal from jam pots.

This year the show was even better than usual, and at the end **tumultuous** applause was given by the dozen girls who crowded in for the performance. The excitement had hardly **subsided** when Hannah appeared, with "Mrs. March's compliments, and would the ladies walk down to supper."

This was a surprise even to the actors, and when they saw the table, they looked at one another in **rapturous** amazement. There was ice cream, cake, fruit, French bonbons and, in the middle of the table, four great bouquets of flowers. It quite took their breath away, and they stared first at the table and then at their mother.

"Old Mr. Laurence sent it," announced Mrs. March.

TRIFLE (<u>try</u> fuhl) *n.*
   1. a thing that is unimportant or not valuable
      Synonym: triviality
   2. a small amount
      Synonyms: bit, touch, tad

CAPITAL (<u>kap</u> uh tuhl) *n.*
   being of the highest category or quality
      Synonyms: exceptional, superior

ACQUAINTED (uh <u>kwayn</u> ted) *adj.*
   having gained knowledge of something
      Synonym: familiar

SATISFACTION (sat iss <u>fak</u> shuhn) *n.*
   a content, happy feeling
      Synonyms: pleasure, approval

"The Laurence boy's grandfather! What in the world put such a thing into his head? We don't know him!" exclaimed Meg.

"Hannah told one of his servants about your breakfast party. That pleased him. He knew my father years ago, and he sent me a note, saying he hoped I would allow him to express his friendly feeling toward my children by sending a few **trifles** in honor of the day. So you have a feast to make up for the bread-and-milk breakfast."

"That boy put it into his head, I know he did! He's a **capital** fellow, and I wish we could get **acquainted**," said Jo, as the plates went round with ohs and ahs of **satisfaction**.

GARRET (<u>gar</u> uht) *n.*
the highest room in a house
Synonyms: attic, loft

HUSKY (<u>huhss</u> kee) *adj.*
low and hoarse
Synonyms: rough, gutteral

INVITATION (in vi <u>tay</u> shuhn) *n.*
a request for someone's presence
Synonyms: call, summons

CHAPTER 3

"Jo! Jo! Where are you?" cried Meg at the foot of the **garret** stairs.

"Here!" answered a **husky** voice from above.

"Such fun! Only see! A regular note of **invitation** from Mrs. Gardiner for tomorrow night!" cried Meg, waving the precious paper and then proceeding to read it with girlish delight.

"'Mrs. Gardiner would be happy to see Miss March and Miss Josephine at a little dance on New Year's Eve.' Marmee is willing we should go, now what *shall* we wear?"

ETERNITY (i <u>turn</u> uh tee) *n.*
  a very long time
    Synonyms: infinity, perpetuity

MORTIFIED (<u>mor</u> ti fyed) *adj.*
  embarrassed or ashamed
    Synonyms: offended, horrified

CRUMPLED (<u>kruhm</u> puhld) *adj.*
  squeezed and crushed
    Synonyms: wrinkled, furrowed

"What's the use of asking that, when you know we shall wear our <u>poplins</u>, because we haven't got anything else?" answered Jo.

"If I only had a silk!" sighed Meg. "Mother says I may when I'm eighteen perhaps, but two years is an **eternity** to wait."

"I'm sure our <u>pops</u> look like silk, and they are nice enough for us. Yours is as good as new, but I forgot the burn and the tear in mine. Whatever shall I do?"

"You must sit still all you can and keep your back out of sight. I shall have a new ribbon for my hair, and Marmee will lend me her little pearl pin, and my gloves will do, though they aren't as nice as I'd like."

"Mine are spoiled with lemonade, and I can't get any new ones, so I shall have to go without," said Jo, who never troubled herself much about dress.

"You *must* have gloves, or I won't go," cried Meg decidedly. "You can't dance without them, and if you don't I should be so **mortified**."

"I can hold them **crumpled** up in my hand, so

PRIM (prim) *adj.*
very formal and proper
Synonyms: neat, orderly

BLITHELY (<u>blyth</u> lee) *adv.*
happily, in a carefree way
Synonyms: merrily, cheerfully

no one will know how stained they are. That's all I can do. No! I'll tell you how we can manage, each wear one good one and carry a bad one. Don't you see?"

"Your hands are bigger than mine, and you will stretch my glove dreadfully," began Meg, whose gloves were a tender point with her.

"Then I'll go without. I don't care what people say!" cried Jo, taking up a book.

"You may have it, you may! Only don't stain it, and do behave nicely. Don't put your hands behind you, or stare, or say 'Christopher Columbus!' will you?"

"Don't worry about me. I'll be as **prim** as I can and not get into any scrapes, if I can help it. Now go and answer your note, and let me finish this splendid story."

So Meg went away to "accept with thanks," look over her dress, and sing **blithely** as she did up her one real lace frill, while Jo finished her story and four apples.

On New Year's Eve the parlor was deserted, for the two younger girls played dressing maids

ABSORBED (uhb <u>zorbed</u>) *adj.*
focused on one thing
Synonyms: engrossed, captivated

PERVADE (pur <u>vayd</u>) *v.* **-ing, -ed**
to spread throughout
Synonyms: permeate

SUPERIOR (suh <u>peer</u> ee uhr) *adj.*
haughty, proud
Synonym: conceited

SCORCHED (skorched) *adj.*
burned or dried up
Synonyms: seared, charred

BUREAU (<u>byur</u> oh) *n.*
a container or chest of drawers
Synonym: dresser

DESPAIR (di <u>spayr</u>) *n.*
the complete loss of hope
Synonyms: hopelessness, misery

and the two elder were **absorbed** in the all-important business of getting ready for the party. Simple as the preparations were, there was a great deal of running up and down, laughing and talking, and at one time a strong smell of burned hair **pervaded** the house. Meg wanted a few curls about her face, and Jo undertook to pinch the locks with some curling papers and a pair of hot tongs.

"Ought they to smoke like that?" asked Beth from her perch on the bed.

"It's the dampness drying," replied Jo.

"What a queer smell! It's like burned feathers," observed Amy, smoothing her own pretty curls with a **superior** <u>air</u>.

"There, you'll see a cloud of little ringlets," said Jo, putting down the tongs and removing the papers.

But no cloud of ringlets appeared, and the horrified hairdresser laid a row of little **scorched** bundles on the **bureau** before her victim.

"Oh, oh, oh! What have you done? I'm spoiled! I can't go! My hair, oh, my hair!" wailed Meg, looking with **despair** at her forehead.

CONSOLINGLY (kuhn <u>sole</u> ihng lee) *adv.*
done with the intent to cheer or comfort
Synonyms: pityingly, soothingly, helpfully

PETULANTLY (<u>pet</u> choo lent lee) *adv.*
done with a sulky and ill-tempered mood
Synonyms: grouchily, irritably

EXERTION (eg <u>zur</u> shuhn) *n.*
effort to do something
Synonyms: action, application

"Just my luck! You shouldn't have asked me to do it. I always spoil everything. I'm so sorry, but the tongs were too hot, and so I've made a mess," groaned poor Jo, regarding the little black pancakes with tears of regret.

"It isn't spoiled. Just tie your ribbon so the ends come on your forehead a bit, and it will look like the latest fashion. I've seen many girls do it so," said Amy **consolingly**.

"Serves me right for trying to be fancy. I wish I'd let my hair alone," cried Meg **petulantly**.

After various lesser mishaps, Meg was finished at last, and by the united **exertions** of the entire family Jo's hair was got up and her dress on. Each put on one nice light glove and carried one soiled one, and all pronounced the effect "quite easy and fine."

"Have a good time, dearies!" said Mrs. March, as the sisters went daintily down the walk. "Don't eat much supper, and come away at eleven when I send Hannah for you."

Once they arrived at Mrs. Gardiner's, the two sisters quickly inspected each other's outfits. "If

JOVIAL (<u>joh</u> vee uhl) *adj.*
cheerful and willing to talk to others
Synonyms: jolly, happy

you see me doing anything wrong," said Jo, "just remind me by a wink, will you?"

"No, winking isn't ladylike. I'll lift my eyebrows if anything is wrong and nod if you are all right. Now hold your shoulder straight and take short steps, and don't shake hands if you are introduced to anyone. It isn't the thing."

"How do you learn all the proper ways? I never can. Isn't that music gay?"

Down they went, feeling a trifle timid, for they seldom went to parties, and informal as this little gathering was, it was an event to them. Mrs. Gardiner, a stately old lady, greeted them kindly and handed them over to the eldest of her six daughters.

Meg knew Sallie and was at her ease very soon, but Jo, who didn't care much for girls or girlish gossip, stood about, with her back carefully against the wall, and felt as much out of place as a colt in a flower garden. Half a dozen **jovial** lads were talking about skates in another part of the room, and she longed to go and join them, for skating was one of the joys of her life. She telegraphed her wish to Meg, but the eyebrows went up so

DWINDLE (<u>dwin</u> duhl) *v.* **-ing**, **-ed**
to become smaller in size or fewer in number
Synonyms: decrease, diminish

FORLORNLY (for <u>lorn</u> lee) *adv.*
displaying loneliness and sadness
Synonyms: pitifully, dejectedly

BRISKLY (<u>brisk</u> lee) *adv.*
done with speed and energy
Synonyms: quickly, rapidly

BASHFUL (<u>bash</u> fuhl) *adj.*
Withdrawn, uncomfortable with people
Synonyms: shy, withdrawn, timid

REFUGE (<u>ref</u> yooj) *n.*
a place that provides shelter and safety
Synonyms: sanctuary, asylum

alarmingly that she dared not stir. No one came to talk to her, and one by one the group **dwindled** away till she was left alone. So she stared at people rather **forlornly** till the dancing began.

Meg was asked to dance at once, and her tight slippers tripped about so **briskly** that none would have guessed the pain their wearer suffered smilingly. Jo saw a big red-headed youth approaching her corner, and fearing he meant to ask her to dance, she slipped behind some curtains, intending to enjoy herself in peace. Unfortunately, another **bashful** person had chosen the same **refuge**, for, as the curtain fell behind her, she found herself face to face with the "Laurence boy."

"Dear me, I didn't know anyone was here!" stammered Jo.

But the boy laughed and said pleasantly, "Don't mind me. Stay if you like. I only came here because I don't know many people and felt rather strange at first, you know."

The boy looked at his shoes, till Jo said, trying to be polite and easy, "I think I've had the pleasure of seeing you before. You live near us, don't you?"

GLISTEN (<u>gliss</u> uhn) *v.* **-ing**, **-ed**
to sparkle or shine
Synonyms: gleam, shimmer

SENTIMENTAL (sent uh <u>men</u> tuhl) *adj.*
evoking emotions or feelings
Synonyms: gushy, sappy

"Next door." And he looked up and laughed outright, for Jo's prim manner was rather funny.

That put Jo at her ease, and she laughed too, as she said, in her heartiest way, "We did have such a good time over your nice Christmas present."

"Grandpa sent it."

"But you put it into his head, didn't you, now?"

"What makes you think that, Miss March?" asked the boy, trying to look sober while his black eyes **glistened** with fun.

"I am not Miss March, I'm only Jo," returned the young lady.

"I'm not Mr. Laurence, I'm only Laurie."

"Laurie Laurence, what an odd name."

"My first name is Theodore, but I don't like it, for the fellows called me Dora, so I made them say Laurie instead. But you can call me Teddy."

"I hate my name, too, so **sentimental**! I wish everyone would say Jo instead of Josephine."

As they talked, Laurie explained that he had been abroad a good many years. "Abroad!" cried Jo. "Oh, tell me about it! I love to hear people describe their travels."

ACQUAINTANCE (uh <u>kwayn</u> tuhns) *n.*
a person who is known
Synonyms: friend, associate

DEMEANOR (duh <u>meen</u> uhr) *n.*
a person's behavior or attitude
Synonyms: conduct, disposition

Laurie didn't seem to know where to begin, but Jo's eager questions soon set him going about his travels and his school in France.

"Did you go to Paris?" cried Jo.

"We spent last winter there."

"Can you talk French?"

"We were not allowed to speak anything else at my school."

"Do say some! I can read it but can't pronounce."

"*Quel nom a cette jeune demoiselle en les pantoufles jolis?*"

"How nicely you do it! Let me see – you said, 'Who is the young lady in the pretty slippers,' didn't you?"

"*Oui, mademoiselle.*"

"It's my sister Margaret, and you knew it was!"

They chatted on till they felt like old **acquaintances**. Laurie's bashfulness soon wore off, for Jo's gentlemanly **demeanor** amused and set him at his ease, and Jo was her merry self again, because nobody lifted their eyebrows at her. She liked the "Laurence boy" better than

TACT (takt) *n.*
use of appropriate speech
Synonyms: discretion, judgment

BECKON (<u>bek</u> uhn) *v.* **-ing**, **-ed**
to signal someone to come over
Synonyms: summon, motion

RELUCTANTLY (ri <u>luhk</u> tuhnt lee) *adv.*
done against one's will
Synonyms: unwillingly, grudgingly

ever and took several good looks at him. I wonder how old he is, she thought.

It was on the tip of Jo's tongue to ask, but she
checked herself in time and, with unusual **tact**,
tried to find out in a roundabout way.

"I suppose you are going to college soon?"

Laurie smiled. "Not for a year or two. I won't
go before seventeen, anyway."

"Aren't you but fifteen?" asked Jo, looking at
the tall lad, whom she had imagined seventeen
already.

"Sixteen, next month."

"How I wish I was going to college! You don't
look as if you liked it."

"I hate it!"

"What do you like?"

"To live in Italy and to enjoy myself in my
own way."

Jo wanted very much to ask what his own
way was, but just then Meg appeared in search of
her sister. She **beckoned**, and Jo **reluctantly** followed her into a side room, where she found her on
a sofa, holding her foot, and looking pale.

WRENCH (rench) *n.*

an injury caused by twisting the body sharply
Synonyms: jerk, yank

OCCUR (uh <u>kur</u>) *v.* **-ing**, **-ed**

to happen or come about
Synonyms: arise, appear

DISMALLY (<u>diz</u> muh lee) *adv.*

in a sad way
Synonyms: gloomily, grimly, bleakly

"I've sprained my ankle. That stupid high heel turned and gave me a sad **wrench**. It aches so, I can hardly stand, and I don't know how I'm ever going to get home," she said, rocking to and fro in pain.

"I don't see what you can do, except get a carriage or stay here all night," answered Jo, Then, softly rubbing the poor ankle she said, "I'll ask Laurie to get a carriage," looking relieved as the idea **occurred** to her.

"Mercy, no!" cried Meg. "As soon as supper is over, watch for Hannah and tell me the minute she comes."

Jo went away to the dining room. Making a dart at the table, she spilled some coffee, thereby making the front of her dress as bad as the back.

"Can I help you?" said a friendly voice. And there was Laurie.

"I was trying to get something for Meg, who is very tired, and someone shook me, and here I am in a nice state," answered Jo, glancing **dismally** from the stained skirt to the coffee-colored glove.

"Too bad! I was looking for someone to give this coffee and ice to. May I take it to your sister?"

INSTALLMENT (in <u>stawl</u> muhnt) *n.*
a portion, helping, or serving of something
Synonyms: segment, episode

OBLIGING (uh <u>blije</u> ing) *adj.*
willing to do favors and be helpful
Synonyms: considerate, accommodating

"Oh, thank you! I'll show you where she is. I don't offer to take it myself, for I should only get into another scrape if I did."

Jo led the way, and, as if used to waiting on ladies, Laurie drew up a little table, brought a second **installment** of coffee and ice for Jo, and was so **obliging** that even particular Meg pronounced him a "nice boy." They had a merry time over the bonbons and were in the midst of a quiet game with two or three other young people who had strayed in when Hannah appeared. Meg forgot her foot and rose so quickly that she was forced to catch hold of Jo, with an exclamation of pain.

"Hush! Don't say anything," she whispered, adding aloud, "It's nothing. I turned my foot a little, that's all," and limped upstairs to put her things on.

Hannah scolded, Meg cried, and Jo was at her wits' end, till she decided to take things into her own hands. Jo was looking round for help when Laurie came up and offered his grandfather's carriage, which had just come for him.

"It's so early! You can't mean to go yet?" began Jo.

MISHAP (<u>miss</u> hap) *n.*
a small accident
Synonym: misfortune

LUXURIOUS (luhk <u>shuh</u> ree uhss) *adj.*
comfortable and well-equipped
Synonyms: lavish, opulent

AUBURN (<u>aw</u> burn) *adj.*
reddish brown
Synonyms: ginger, ruddy

"I always go early, I do, truly! Please let me take you home. It's all on my way, you know, and it rains, they say."

That settled it, and telling him of Meg's **mishap**, Jo gratefully accepted and rushed up to bring down the rest of the party. Hannah hated rain as much as a cat does so she made no trouble, and they rolled away in the **luxurious** closed carriage, feeling very festive and elegant. Laurie went to sit on top of the carriage so Meg could keep her foot up, and the girls talked over their party in freedom.

"I had a capital time. Did you?" asked Jo, rumpling up her hair and making herself comfortable.

"Yes, till I hurt myself. Sallie's friend, Annie Moffat, asked me to come and spend a week with her when Sallie does. It will be perfectly splendid," answered Meg, cheering up at the thought.

"I saw you dancing with the red-headed man I ran away from. Was he nice?"

"Oh, very! His hair is **auburn**, not red, and he was very polite.

"He looked like a grasshopper in a fit. Laurie and I couldn't help laughing. Did you hear us?"

"No, but it was very rude. What were you about all that time, hidden away there?"

Jo told her adventures, and by the time she had finished they were at home. With many thanks, they said good night and crept in, hoping to disturb no one. But the instant their door creaked, two little nightcaps bobbed up, and two sleepy but eager voices cried out, "Tell about the party! Tell about the party!"

After hearing the most thrilling events of the evening, the two younger sisters soon subsided. "I declare, it really seems like being a fine young lady, to come home from the party in a carriage and sit in my dressing gown with a maid to wait on me," said Meg, as Jo bound up her foot with <u>arnica</u> and brushed her hair.

"I don't believe fine young ladies enjoy themselves a bit more than we do, in spite of our burned hair, old gowns, one glove apiece and tight slippers that sprain our ankles when we are silly enough to wear them." And I think Jo was quite right.

MISCHIEVOUS (miss <u>chee</u> vee uhss) *adj.*
  playfully troublesome or bad
    Synonyms: naughty, impish

ADVISE (ad <u>vize</u>) *v.* **-ing**, **-ed**
  to suggest or instruct
    Synonyms: counsel, inform

CHAPTER 4

"What in the world are you going to do now, Jo?" asked Meg one snowy afternoon, as her sister came tramping through the hall, in rubber boots, old sack, and hood, with a broom in one hand and a shovel in the other.

"Going out for exercise," answered Jo with a **mischievous** twinkle in her eyes.

"I should think two long walks this morning would have been enough! It's cold and dull out, and I **advise** you to stay warm and dry by the fire, as I do," said Meg with a shiver.

SEPARATE (<u>sep</u> uh rate) *v.* **-ing**, **-ed**
    to part or divide people or things
        Synonyms: split, detach

SUBURB (<u>suhb</u> urb) *n.*
    an area close to or on the edge of a city
        Synonyms: town, district

ENCHANTED (en <u>chan</u> tid) *adj.*
    a person or place put under a magic spell
        Synonyms: charmed, supernatural

"Never take advice! Can't keep still all day, and not being a pussycat, I don't like to doze by the fire. I like adventures, and I'm going to find some."

Meg went back to toast her feet and read, and Jo began to dig paths with great energy. The snow was light, and with her broom she soon swept a path all round the garden for Beth to walk in when the sun came out and the dolls needed air. Now, the garden **separated** the Marches' house from that of Mr. Laurence. Both stood in a **suburb** of the city, which was still countrylike, with groves and lawns, large gardens, and quiet streets. A low hedge parted the two properties.

Yet it seemed a lonely, lifeless sort of house, for no children frolicked on the lawn, no motherly face ever smiled at the windows, and few people went in and out, except the old gentleman and his grandson.

To Jo's lively fancy, this fine house seemed a kind of **enchanted** palace, full of delights which no one enjoyed. She had long wanted to behold these hidden glories and to know the Laurence boy, who looked as if he would like to be known.

The idea amused Jo, who liked to do daring

SCANDALIZE (<u>skan</u> duh lize) *v.* **-ing**, **-ed**
 to shock people through improper behavior
  Synonyms: outrage, dismay

RESOLVE (ri <u>zolv</u>) *v.* **-ing**, **-ed**
 to decide to try to do a certain thing
  Synonyms: determine, conclude

SALLY (<u>sal</u> ee) *v.* **-ing**, **-ed**
 to take a trip, to go toward a destination
  Synonyms: walk, travel

SURVEY (<u>sur</u> vay) *n.*
 a careful examination of something
  Synonyms: review, analysis, look

VISIBLE (<u>viz</u> uh buhl) *adj.*
 able to be spotted or seen
  Synonyms: noticeable, evident

FLOURISH (<u>flur</u> ish) *v.* **-ing**, **-ed**
 to wave something around
  Synonyms: flaunt, display

things and was always **scandalizing** Meg by her queer performances. The plan of "going over" was not forgotten. And when the snowy afternoon came, Jo **resolved** to try what could be done. She saw Mr. Lawrence drive off and then **sallied** out to dig her way down to the hedge, where she paused and took a **survey**. All quiet, curtains down at the lower windows, servants out of sight, and nothing human **visible** but a curly black head leaning on a thin hand at the upper window.

"There he is," thought Jo. "Poor boy! All alone and sick this dismal day. It's a shame! I'll toss up a snowball and make him look out and then say a kind word to him."

Up went a handful of soft snow, and the head turned at once, showing a face which lost its listless look in a minute, as the big eyes brightened and the mouth began to smile. Jo nodded and laughed and **flourished** her broom as she called out, "How do you do? Are you sick?"

Laurie opened the window and croaked out as hoarsely as a raven, "Better, thank you. I've had a bad cold, and been shut up a week."

TOMB (toom) *n.*
    a grave or dark room that holds a dead body
        Synonym: mausoleum

ENTERTAIN (en tur <u>tayn</u>) *v.* **-ing**, **-ed**
    to amuse someone or keep someone busy
        Synonyms: occupy, divert

CONSENT (kuhn <u>sent</u>) *v.* **-ing**, **-ed**
    to agree to something
        Synonyms: approve, allow

"I'm sorry. What do you amuse yourself with?"

"Nothing. It's dull as **tombs** up here."

"Don't you read?"

"Not much. They won't let me."

"Can't somebody read to you?"

"Grandpa does sometimes, but my books don't interest him, and I hate to ask Brooke all the time."

"Have someone come and see you then."

"There isn't anyone I'd like to see. Boys make such a row, and my head hurts."

"Isn't there some nice girl who'd read and **entertain** you? Girls are quiet and like to play nurse."

"Don't know any."

"You know us," began Jo, then laughed and stopped.

"So I do! Will you come, please?" cried Laurie.

"I'm not quiet and nice, but I'll come, if Mother will **consent**. I'll go ask her. Shut the window, like a good boy, and wait till I come."

With that, Jo shouldered her broom and marched into the house, wondering what they

PATE (pate) *n.*
   the top part of a person's skull
      Synonyms: head, scalp

TIDY (<u>tie</u> dee) *v.* **-ing**, **-ed**
   to arrange
      Synonyms: neaten, straighten up

EASE (eez) *n.*
   a calm state of mind
      Synonyms: relaxation, comfort

would all say to her. Laurie was in a flutter of excitement at the idea of having company and flew about to get ready, for as Mrs. March said, he was "a little gentleman" and did honor to the coming guest by brushing his curly **pate**, putting on a fresh color, and trying to **tidy** up the room, which, in spite of half a dozen servants, was anything but neat. Presently there came a loud ring, then a decided voice, asking for "Mr. Laurie," and a surprised-looking servant came running up to announce a young lady.

"All right, show her up, it's Miss Jo," said Laurie, going to the door of his little parlor to meet Jo, who appeared, looking rosy and quite at her **ease**, with a covered dish in one hand and Beth's three kittens in the other.

"Here I am, bag and baggage," she said briskly. "Mother sent her love and was glad if I could do anything for you. Meg wanted me to bring some of her <u>blancmange</u>, she makes it very nicely, and Beth thought her cats would be comforting. I knew you'd laugh at them, but I couldn't refuse, she was so anxious to do something."

LOAN (lohn) *n.*
the act of lending something to someone
Synonyms: advance, mortgage

SOCIABLE (<u>soh</u> shuh buhl) *adj.*
acting in a friendly way
Synonyms: jovial, gregarious

PLEASURE (<u>plezh</u> ur) *n.*
the feeling of being happy or content
Synonyms: joy, delight

It so happened that Beth's funny **loan** was just the thing, for in laughing over the kits, Laurie forgot his shyness and grew **sociable** at once.

"That looks too pretty to eat," he said, smiling with **pleasure**, as Jo uncovered the dish, and showed the blancmange, surrounded by a garland of green leaves, and the scarlet flowers of Amy's pet geranium.

"It isn't anything, only they all felt kindly and wanted to show it. Tell the girl to put it away for your tea. It's so simple you can eat it, and being soft, it will slip down without hurting your sore throat. What a cozy room this is!"

"It might be if it was kept nice, but the maids are lazy, and I don't know how to make them mind. It worries me though."

"I'll right it up in two minutes, for it only needs to have the hearth brushed, so – and the things made straight on the mantelpiece, so – and the books put here, and the bottles there, and your sofa turned from the light, and the pillows plumped up a bit. Now then, you're fixed."

And so he was, for, as she laughed and

RESPECTFUL (ri <u>spekt</u> fuhl) *adj.*
giving proper courtesy and consideration
Synonyms: polite, civil

AMUSE (uh <u>myooz</u>) *v.* **-ing**, **-ed**
to keep someone from being bored
Synonyms: entertain, occupy

AFFECTIONATELY (uh <u>fek</u> shuh nuht lee) *adv.*
done in a caring way
Synonyms: lovingly, warmly, tenderly

talked, Jo had whisked things into place and given quite a different air to the room. Laurie watched her in **respectful** silence, and when she beckoned him to his sofa, he sat down with a sigh of satisfaction, saying gratefully, "How kind you are! Yes, that's what it wanted. Now please, take the big chair and let me do something to **amuse** my company."

"No, I came to amuse you. Shall I read aloud?" and Jo looked **affectionately** toward some inviting books nearby.

"Thank you! I've read all those, and if you don't mind, I'd rather talk," answered Laurie.

"Not a bit. I'll talk all day if you'll only set me going. Beth says I never know when to stop."

"Is Beth the rosy one, who stays at home a good deal and sometimes goes out with a little basket?" asked Laurie with interest.

"Yes, that's Beth. She's my girl, and a regular good one she is, too, though being sick so often she doesn't get out much."

"The pretty one is Meg, and the curly-haired one is Amy, I believe?"

"How did you find that out?"

FRANKLY (<u>frank</u> lee) *adv.*
openly and honestly
Synonyms: bluntly, candidly

ILLUMINATED (i <u>loom</u> uh nay ted) *adj.*
bright
Synonym: lit

SOLITARY (<u>sahl</u> uh ter ee) *adj.*
spending a lot of time alone
Synonyms: lonely, isolated

INNOCENT (<u>in</u> uh suhnt) *adj.*
unknowing, guiltless
Synonyms: blameless, simple

Laurie colored up, but answered **frankly**, "Why, you see I often hear you calling to one another, and when I'm alone up here I can't help looking over at your house. You always seem to be having such good times. I beg your pardon for being so rude, but sometimes you forget to put down the curtain at the window where the flowers are. And when the lamps are **illuminated**, it's like looking at a picture to see the fire and you all around the table with your mother. Her face is right opposite me, and she looks so sweet behind the flowers, I can't help watching it. I haven't got any mother, you know." And Laurie poked the fire to hide a little twitching of the lips that he could not control.

The **solitary**, hungry look in his eyes went straight to Jo's warm heart. She had been so simply taught that there was no nonsense in her head, and at fifteen she was as **innocent** and frank as any child. Laurie was sick and lonely, and feeling how rich she was in home and happiness, she gladly tried to share it with him. Her face was very friendly and her sharp voice unusually gentle as

PROPERTY (<u>prop</u> ur tee) *n.*

    1. a special characteristic or quality of something

        Synonyms: aspect, feature

    2. an object used onstage

        Synonym: prop

ACQUAINT (uh <u>kwaynt</u>) *v.* **-ing**, **-ed**

    1. to cause to know personally

        Synonym: introduce

    2. to make familiar or aware

        Synonyms: explain, inform

she said, "We'll never draw that curtain anymore, and I give you leave to look as much as you like. I just wish, though, instead of peeping, you'd come over and see us. Mother is so splendid, she'd do you heaps of good, and Beth would sing to you if I begged her to, and Amy would dance. Meg and I would make you laugh over our funny stage **properties**, and we'd have jolly times. Wouldn't your grandpa let you?"

"I think he would, if your mother asked him. He's very kind, though he does not look so, and he lets me do what I like, pretty much, only he's afraid I might be a bother to strangers," began Laurie, brightening more and more.

"We are not strangers, we are neighbors, and you needn't think you'd be a bother. We want to know you, and I've been trying to do this ever so long. We haven't been here a great while, you know, but we have got **acquainted** with all our neighbors but you."

"You see, Grandpa lives among his books, and doesn't mind much what happens outside. Mr. Brooke, my tutor, doesn't stay here, you know, and

BLUNT (bluhnt) *adj.*
straightforward and honest
Synonyms: frank, candid

INQUIRY (<u>in</u> kwuh ree) *n.*
investigation or study
Synonyms: examination, exploration

AFFAIRS (uh <u>fayrz</u>) *n.*
matters and business in people's lives
Synonyms: dealings, interactions

I have no one to go about with me, so I just stop at home and get on as I can."

"That's bad. You ought to make an effort and go visiting everywhere you are asked, and then you'll have plenty of friends and pleasant places to go to. Never mind being bashful. It won't last long if you keep going."

Laurie turned red again but wasn't offended at being accused of bashfulness, for there was so much good will in Jo it was impossible not to take her **blunt** speeches as kindly as they were meant.

"Do you like your school?" asked the boy, changing the subject after a little pause, during which he stared at the fire and Jo looked about her, well pleased.

"Don't go to school, I'm a businessman – girl, I mean. I go to wait on my great-aunt, and a dear, cross old soul she is, too," answered Jo.

Laurie opened his mouth to ask another question, but remembering just in time that it wasn't manners to make too many **inquiries** into people's **affairs**, he shut it again and looked uncomfortable.

DESCRIPTION (di <u>skrip</u> shuhn) *n.*
   an observation or account of something
   Synonyms: explanation, report

REVEL (<u>rev</u> uhl) *v.* **-ing**, **-ed**
   to take pleasure or enjoyment from something
   Synonyms: bask, relish

MERRIMENT (<u>mer</u> ee muhnt) *n.*
   happiness and fun
   Synonyms: jollity, glee

ELATED (i <u>lay</u> tid) *adj.*
   excited and happy
   Synonyms: thrilled, ecstatic

Jo liked his good <u>breeding</u>, and didn't mind having a laugh at Aunt March, so she gave him a lively **description** of the old lady, her fat poodle, the parrot that talked Spanish, and the library where she **reveled**.

Laurie enjoyed that a lot, and when she told about the proper old gentleman who came once to woo Aunt March, and in the middle of a fine speech, how Poll had pulled his wig off to his great dismay, the boy lay back and laughed till the tears ran down his cheeks and a maid popped her head in to see what was the matter.

"Oh! That does me no end of good. Tell on, please," he said, taking his face out of the sofa cushion, red and shining with **merriment**.

Much **elated** with her success, Jo did "tell on," all about their plays and plans, their hopes and fears for Father, and the most interesting events of the little world in which the sisters lived. Then they got to talking about books, and to Jo's delight, she found that Laurie loved them as much as she did and had read even more than herself.

"If you like them so much, come down and

ADMIRATION (ad mir <u>ay</u> shuhn) *n.*
approval and high regard
Synonyms: respect, esteem

ESPECIALLY (ess <u>pesh</u> uh lee) *adv.*
more than normally, particularly
Synonyms: strongly, powerfully

DISTRACTING (diss <u>trakt</u> ing) *adj.*
taking attention away from something else
Synonyms: disturbing, mesmerizing

QUAINT (kwaynt) *adj.*
antique, charming
Synonyms: picturesque, old-fashioned

VELOUR (vuh <u>loor</u>) *n.*
a thick, soft fabric
Synonym: velvet

see ours. Grandfather is out, so you needn't be afraid," said Laurie, getting up.

"I'm not afraid of anything," returned Jo, with a toss of the head.

"I don't believe you are!" exclaimed the boy, looking at her with much **admiration**, though he privately thought she would have good reason to be a trifle afraid of the old gentleman, if she met him in some of his moods.

The atmosphere of the whole house being summerlike, Laurie led the way from room to room, letting Jo stop to examine whatever struck her fancy. And so at last they came to the library, where she clapped her hands and pranced, as she always did when **especially** delighted. It was lined with books, and there were pictures and statues and **distracting** little cabinets full of coins and curiosities, and fancy chairs, and odd tables, and bronzes, and best of all, a great open fireplace with **quaint** tiles all round it.

"What richness!" sighed Jo, sinking into the depth of a **velour** chair and gazing about her with an air of satisfaction. "Theodore Laurence, you

IMPRESSIVELY (im <u>press</u> iv lee) *adv.*
   done so well as to gain the respect of others
   Synonyms: remarkably, notably

COMPOSE (kuhm <u>poze</u>) *v.* **-ing**, **-ed**
   to become calm
   Synonyms: level, settle

ought to be the happiest boy in the world," she added **impressively**.

"A fellow can't live on books," said Laurie, shaking his head as he perched on a table opposite.

Before he could move, a bell rang, and Jo flew up, exclaiming with alarm, "Mercy me! It's your grandpa!"

"Well, what if it is? You are not afraid of anything, you know," returned the boy, looking wicked.

"I think I am a little bit afraid of him, but I don't know why I should be. Marmee said I might come, and I don't think you're any the worse for it," said Jo, **composing** herself, though she kept her eyes on the door.

"I'm a great deal better for it and ever so much obliged. I'm only afraid you are very tired of talking to me. It was so pleasant, I couldn't bear to stop," said Laurie gratefully.

"The doctor to see you, sir," and the maid beckoned as she spoke.

"Would you mind if I left you for a minute? I suppose I must see him," said Laurie.

PORTRAIT (<u>por</u> trit) *n.*
a picture of someone
Synonyms: likeness, painting, drawing

TREMENDOUS (tri <u>men</u> duhss) *adj.*
very large, big
Synonyms: great, immense

DISMAY (diss <u>may</u>) *n.*
Worry or sadness
Synonyms: distress, alarm

POSSESS (puh <u>zess</u>) *v.* **-ing**, **-ed**
to influence or take control of
Synonyms: seize, acquire

RESOLVE (rih <u>zolv</u>) *v.* **-ing**, **-ed**
to make up one's mind
Synonyms: decide, determine

"Don't mind me. I'm happy as a cricket here," answered Jo.

Laurie went away, and his guest amused herself in her own way. She was standing before a fine **portrait** of the old gentleman when the door opened again, and without turning, she said decidedly, "I'm sure now that I shouldn't be afraid of him, for he's got kind eyes, though his mouth is grim, and he looks as if he had a **tremendous** will of his own. He isn't as handsome as my grandfather, but I like him."

"Thank you, ma'am," said a gruff voice behind her, and there, to her great **dismay**, stood old Mr. Laurence.

Poor Jo blushed till she couldn't blush any redder, and her heart began to beat uncomfortably fast as she thought of what she had said. For a minute a wild desire to run away **possessed** her, but that was cowardly, and the girls would laugh at her, so she **resolved** to stay and get out of the scrape as best she could. A second look showed her that the living eyes, under the bushy eyebrows, were kinder even than the painted ones, and there was a sly

ABRUPTLY (uh <u>brupt</u> lee) *adv.*
   in a quick or sudden way
      Synonyms: quickly, shortly, brusquely

GRAVELY (<u>grayv</u> lee) *adv.*
   very seriously
      Synonyms: sternly, grimly

twinkle in them, which lessened her fear a good deal. The gruff voice was gruffer than ever, as the old gentleman said **abruptly**, after the dreadful pause, "So you're not afraid of me, hey?"

"Not much, sir."

"And you don't think me as handsome as your grandfather?"

"Not quite, sir."

"And I've got a tremendous will, have I?"

"I only said I thought so."

"But you like me anyway?"

"Yes, I do, sir."

That answer pleased the old gentleman. He gave a short laugh, shook hands with her, and, putting his finger under her chin, turned up her face, examined it **gravely**, and let it go, saying with a nod, "You've got your grandfather's spirit, if you haven't his face. He was a fine man, my dear, but what is better, he was a brave and an honest one, and I was proud to be his friend."

"Thank you, sir," and Jo was quite comfortable after that, for it suited her exactly.

NEIGHBORLY (<u>nay</u> bur lee) *adj.*
kind, helpful, sociable to one's neighbor
Synonyms: considerate, helpful

MARVELOUS (<u>mar</u> vuh luhss) *adj.*
causing much surprise and amazement
Synonyms: stunning, wonderful

ACCOUNT (uh <u>kount</u>) *n.*
for the sake of, by reason of
Synonyms: behalf, benefit

"What have you been doing to this boy of mine, hey?" was the next question, sharply put.

"Only trying to be **neighborly**, sir." And Jo told how her visit came about.

"You think he needs cheering up a bit, do you?"

"Yes, sir, he seems a little lonely, and young folks would do him good perhaps. We girls should be glad to help if we could, for we don't forget the **marvelous** Christmas present you sent us," said Jo eagerly.

"Tut, tut, tut! That was the boy's affair. How is the poor woman?"

"Doing nicely, sir." And off went Jo, talking very fast, as she told all about the Hummels, in whom her mother had interested richer friends than they were.

"Just her father's way of doing good. I shall come and see your mother some fine day. Tell her so. There's the tea bell. We have it early on the boy's **account**. Come down and go on being neighborly."

"If you'd like to have me, sir."

"Shouldn't ask you, if I didn't." And

REDOUBTABLE (ri <u>dowt</u> uh buhl) *adj.*
worthy of fear and respect
Synonyms: impressive, formidable

TRIUMPHANT (try <u>uhm</u> fuhnt) *adj.*
victorious or successful
Synonyms: glorious, exultant

EVIDENT (<u>ev</u> uh duhnt) *adj.*
made obvious and clear
Synonyms: apparent, lucid

CARESS (kuh <u>ress</u>) *n.*
a caring touch or embrace
Synonyms: stroke, pat

EXPLOSION (ek <u>sploh</u> zhuhn) *n.*
a noisy release of something
Synonyms: blast, outburst

Mr. Laurence offered her his arm with old-fashioned courtesy.

"What would Meg say to this?" thought Jo, as she was marched away, while her eyes danced with fun as she imagined herself telling the story at home.

"Hey! Why, what the dickens has come to the fellow?" said the old gentleman, as Laurie came running downstairs and brought up with a start of surprise at the sight of Jo arm in arm with his **redoubtable** grandfather.

"I didn't know you'd come, sir," he began, as Jo gave him a **triumphant** little glance.

"That's **evident** by the way you racket downstairs. Come to your tea, sir, and behave like a gentleman." And having pulled the boy's hair by way of a **caress**, Mr. Laurence walked on, while Laurie went through a series of comic movements behind their backs, which nearly produced an **explosion** of laughter from Jo.

The old gentleman stood in another room and did not say much as he drank his four cups of tea, but he watched the young people, who soon

VIVACITY (vi <u>vass</u> i tee) *n.*
 liveliness and cheerfulness
  Synonyms: energy, exuberance

GENUINE (<u>jen</u> yoo uhn) *adj.*
 true and honest
  Synonyms: real, authentic

EXPRESSION (ek <u>spresh</u> uhn) *n.*
 the display of one's feelings on one's face
  Synonyms: look, appearance

MODESTLY (<u>mod</u> ist lee) *adv.*
 without bragging or boasting
  Synonyms: humbly, meekly

chatted away like old friends, and the change in his grandson did not escape him. There was color, light, and life in the boy's face now, **vivacity** in his manner, and **genuine** happiness in his laugh.

After a while, Laurie took Jo off to the <u>conservatory</u>, where she marveled at the vines and trees and flowers. Her new friend cut her the finest flowers until his hands were full. "Please, give these to your mother, and tell her I like the medicine she has sent me," he declared.

When they returned from the conservatory, they found Mr. Laurence standing before the fire in the great drawing room, but Jo's attention was absorbed by a grand piano, which stood open.

"Do you play?" she asked, turning to Laurie with a respectful **expression**.

"Sometimes," he answered **modestly**.

"Please do now. I want to hear it, so I can tell Beth."

"Won't you first?"

"Don't know how. Too stupid to learn, but I love music dearly."

So Laurie played and Jo listened, with her

REGARD (ri <u>gard</u>) *n.*
an attitude toward someone or something
Synonym: opinion

ABASHED (uh <u>bashd</u>) *adj.*
ill at ease, feeling guilty or unworthy
Synonym: embarrassed

AMISS (uh <u>miss</u>) *adv.*
wrong or incorrect
Synonyms: mistaken, muddled

nose luxuriously buried in tea roses. Her respect and **regard** for the "Laurence boy" increased very much, for he played remarkably well and didn't put on any airs. She wished Beth could hear him, but she did not say so, only praised him till he was quite **abashed**, and his grandfather came to his rescue.

"That will do, that will do, young lady. Too many sugarplums are not good for him. His music isn't bad, but I hope he will do as well in more important things. Going? Well, I'm much obliged to you, and I hope you'll come again. My respects to your mother. Good night, Doctor Jo."

He shook hands kindly but looked as if something did not please him. When they got into the hall, Jo asked Laurie if she had said something **amiss**. He shook his head.

"No, it was me. He doesn't like to hear me play."

"Why not?"

"I'll tell you someday. John is going home with you, as I can't."

"No need of that. I am not a young lady, and it's only a step. Take care of yourself, won't you?"

"Yes, but you will come again, I hope?"

INCLINED (in <u>klynd</u>) *adj.*
   liking or tending to do something
     Synonyms: liable, prone

ATTRACTIVE (uh <u>trak</u> tiv) *adj.*
   interesting or pretty to observe
     Synonyms: appealing, tempting

DISPOSITION (diss puh <u>zish</u> uhn) *n.*
   a leaning to behave a certain way
     Synonyms: nature, character

ACCOMPLISHED (uh <u>kom</u> plisht) *adj.*
   skilled and having much talent
     Synonyms: gifted, proficient

"If you promise to come and see us after you are well."

"I will."

"Good night, Laurie!"

"Good night, Jo, good night!"

When all the afternoon's adventures had been told, the family felt **inclined** to go visiting in a body, for each found something very **attractive** in the big house on the other side of the hedge. Mrs. March wanted to talk of her father with the old man who had not forgotten him, Meg longed to walk in the conservatory, Beth sighed for the grand piano, and Amy was eager to see the fine pictures and statues.

"Mother, why didn't Mr. Laurence like to have Laurie play?" asked Jo, who was of a questioning **disposition**.

"I am not sure, but I think it was because his son, Laurie's father, married an Italian lady, a musician, which displeased the old man, who is very proud. The lady was good and lovely and **accomplished**, but he did not like her, and never saw his son after he married. They both died when

NATURALLY (<u>nach</u> ur uh lee) *adv.*
    having been given or endowed since birth
        Synonym: innately

GLOWER (<u>glou</u> ur) *v.* **-ing**, **-ed**
    to stare angrily
        Synonyms: glare, frown

Laurie was a little child, and then his grandfather took him home. I fancy the boy, who was born in Italy, is not very strong, and the old man is afraid of losing him, which makes him so careful. Laurie comes **naturally** by his love of music, for he is like his mother, and I dare say his grandfather fears that he may want to be a musician. At any rate, his skill reminds him of the woman he did not like, and so he '**glowered**' as Jo said."

"Dear me, how romantic!" exclaimed Meg.

"How silly!" said Jo. "Let him be a musician if he wants to, and not plague his life out sending him to college, when he hates to go. We'll all be good to him because he hasn't got any mother, and he may come over and see us, mayn't he, Marmee?"

"Yes, Jo, your little friend is very welcome."

INFORM (in <u>form</u>) *v.* **-ing**, **-ed**
   to give information
      Synonyms: notify, advise

CHAPTER 5

The big house did prove a Palace Beautiful, though it took time for all of the Marches to get there. All sorts of pleasant things happened about that time, for the new friendship flourished like grass in spring. Everyone liked Laurie, and he privately **informed** his tutor that "the Marches were regularly splendid girls." With the delightful enthusiasm of youth, they took the solitary boy under their wing.

What good times they had, to be sure. Such plays, such sleigh rides and skating frolics, such

VORACIOUSLY (vor <u>ay</u> shuss lee) *adv.*
　very enthusiastically, with great appetite
　　Synonyms: hungrily, ravenously, eagerly

CONVULSE (kuhn <u>vulss</u>) *v.* **-ing**, **-ed**
　to cause someone to laugh strongly
　　Synonym: amuse

CRITICISM (<u>krit</u> uh siz uhm) *n.*
　opinion or judgment of others
　　Synonyms: assessment, critique

PERUSASION (pur <u>sway</u> zhun) *n.*
　attempt to convince someone to do something
　　Synonyms: urge, appeal

ENTICEMENT (en <u>tyss</u> muhnt) *n.*
　something encouraging someone to take action
　　Synonyms: incentive, attraction

NEGLECT (ni <u>glekt</u>) *v.* **-ing**, **-ed**
　to not take care of or pay attention to something
　　Synonyms: ignore, disregard

pleasant evenings in the old parlor, and now and then such gay little parties at the great house. Meg could walk in the conservatory whenever she liked and revel in flowers, Jo browsed over the new library **voraciously** and **convulsed** the old gentleman with her **criticisms**, Amy copied pictures and enjoyed beauty to her heart's content, and Laurie played lord of the manor in the most delightful style.

But Beth, though yearning for the grand piano, could not pluck up courage to go to the "Mansion of Bliss" as Meg called it. No **persuasions** or **enticements** could overcome her fear, till, the fact coming to Mr. Laurence's ear in some mysterious way, he set about mending matters. During one of the brief calls he made, he artfully led the conversation to music.

At the back of his chair Beth stopped and stood listening, and as if the idea had just occurred to him, he said to Mrs. March, "The boy **neglects** his music now, and I'm glad of it, for he was getting too fond of it. But the piano suffers for want of use. Wouldn't some of your girls like to

ARRANGEMENT (uh raynj muhnt) *n.*
a plan or agreement
Synonyms: concurrence, understanding

GRATITUDE (<u>grat</u> uh tood) *n.*
thankfulness
Synonyms: thanks, appreciation

OBLIGED (uh <u>blyjd</u>) *adj.*
thankful and indebted
Synonym: grateful

run over and practice on it now and then, just to keep it in tune, you know, ma'am?"

"Really?" replied Beth, looking at Mr. Lawrence.

"They needn't see or speak to anyone but simply run in at any time and play."

Here he rose, as if going, and Beth overcame her shyness and made up her mind to speak, for the **arrangement** he proposed was perfect for her.

"Please, tell the young ladies what I say," Mr. Laurence concluded, "and if they don't care to come, why, never mind." Here a little hand slipped into his, and Beth looked up at him with a face full of **gratitude**, as she said, in her serious yet timid way, "Oh sir, they do care, very very much!"

"Are you the musical girl?" he asked.

"I'm Beth. I love music dearly, and I'll come, if you are quite sure nobody will be disturbed," she added, fearing to be rude and trembling at her own boldness as she spoke.

"Not a soul, my dear. The house is empty half the day, so come and drum away as much as you like, and I shall be **obliged** to you."

BENEFIT (<u>ben</u> uh fit) *n.*
something that will do someone good
Synonyms: profit, gain

DISCUSSION (diss <u>kush</u> uhn) *n.*
a talk between people
Synonyms: conversation, debate

"How kind you are, sir!"

"I had a little girl once, with eyes like these. God bless you, my dear! Good day, madam." And away he went, in a great hurry.

After that, the little girl slipped through the hedge nearly every day, and the great drawing room was haunted by a tuneful spirit that came and went unseen. She never knew she reminded Mr. Laurence of a granddaughter who had died long ago. Nor did she know that Mr. Laurence opened his study door to hear the old-fashioned airs he liked. She never saw Laurie mount guard in the hall to warn the servants away. She never suspected that the exercise books and new songs which she found in the rack were put there for her **benefit**. "Can I make Mr. Laurence a pair of slippers for being so kind?" asked Beth of her mother.

"Yes, dear. It will please him very much and be a nice way of thanking him."

After many serious **discussions** with Meg and Jo, the pattern was chosen, the materials bought, and the slippers begun. A cluster of grave yet cheerful flowers on a deeper purple ground was

PRONOUNCE (pruh <u>nounss</u>) *v.* **-ing**, **-ed**
to state firmly
Synonym: declare

APPROPRIATE (uh <u>proh</u> pree uht) *adj.*
correct and suitable for a situation
Synonyms: right, proper

GESTICULATE (jess <u>tik</u> yuh layt) *v.* **-ing**, **-ed**
to gesture with one's hands
Synonyms: wave, signal

SUSPENSE (suh <u>spenss</u>) *n.*
a feeling that something important or
unpleasant will happen
Synonyms: anticipation, anxiety

pronounced very **appropriate** and pretty, and Beth worked away early and late, with occasional help on hard parts. She was a fine little needlewoman, and they were finished before anyone got tired of them. Then she wrote a short, simple note and with Laurie's help got them smuggled onto the study table one morning before the old gentleman was up.

After some waiting, the sisters received a response from the old man.

"Oh, Beth, he's sent you—" began Amy, **gesticulating** with unseemly energy at what had just been brought into the house. But she got no further, for Jo stopped her by slamming down the window.

Beth hurried toward the door in a flutter of **suspense**. Before she got there her sisters grabbed and brought her to the parlor in a great procession, all pointing and all saying at once, "Look there! Look there!"

Beth did look, and she turned pale with delight and surprise. For there stood a little piano, with a letter lying on the glossy lid, directed like a sign board to "Miss Elizabeth March."

PROVIDER (pro <u>vy</u> dur) *n.*
one who supplies something
Synonyms: source, contributor

"For me?" gasped Beth, holding onto Jo and feeling as if she should tumble down, it was such an overwhelming thing altogether.

"Yes, all for you, my precious! Isn't it splendid of him? Don't you think he's the dearest old man in the world? Here's the key in the letter. We are all dying to know what he says," cried Jo, hugging her sister and offering the note.

"You read it! I can't, I feel so odd! Oh, it is too lovely!" and Beth hid her face in Jo's apron, quite upset by her present.

Jo opened the paper and began to laugh, for the first words she saw were:

Miss March: Dear Madam—

"How nice it sounds! I wish someone would write to me so!" said Amy, who thought the old-fashioned address very elegant. Jo continued to read the letter aloud:

I have had many pairs of slippers in my life, but I never had any that suited me so well as yours. Heartsease is my favorite flower, and these will always remind me of the gentle **provider**. I like

PACIFY (<u>pass</u> uh fy) *v.* **-ing**, **-ed**
to calm someone down
Synonyms: soothe, appease, propitiate

PUCKER (<u>puh</u> kur) *v.* **-ing**, **-ed**
to make small wrinkles and creases
Synonyms: ruffle, scrunch

to pay my debts, so I know you will allow "the old gentleman" to send you something which once belonged to the little granddaughter he lost. With hearty thanks and best wishes, I remain

Your grateful friend and humble servant,
JAMES LAURENCE

"There, Beth, that's an honor to be proud of, I'm sure! Laurie told me how fond Mr. Laurence used to be of the child who died, and how he kept all her little things carefully. Just think, he's given you her piano. That comes of having big blue eyes and loving music," said Jo, trying to **pacify** Beth, who trembled and looked more excited than she had ever been before.

"See the brackets to hold candles, and the nice green silk, **puckered** up, with a gold rose in the middle, and the pretty rack and stool, all complete," added Meg, opening the instrument and displaying its beauties.

"'Your humble servant, James Laurence.' Only think of his writing that to you. I'll tell the girls. They'll think it's splendid," said Amy, much impressed by the note.

"You'll have to go and thank him," said Jo, by

DELIBERATELY (duh <u>lib</u> ur uht lee) *adv.*
done in a careful, thoughtful way
Synonyms: purposely, consciously

QUEEREST (<u>kweer</u> uhst) *adj.*
most unusual
Synonyms: strangest, oddest, weirdest

RENDER (<u>ren</u> dur) *v.* **-ing**, **-ed**
1. to cause or to make
Synonym: force
2. to give
Synonym: provide

way of a joke, for the idea of the child's really going never entered her head.

"Yes, I mean to. I guess I'll go now, before I get frightened thinking about it." And, to the utter amazement of the assembled family, Beth walked **deliberately** down the garden, through the hedge, and in at the Laurences' door.

"Well, I wish I may die if it ain't the **queerest** thing I ever see! The pianny has turned her head! She'd never have gone in her right mind," cried Hannah, staring after her, while the girls were **rendered** quite speechless by the miracle.

They would have been still more amazed if they had seen what Beth did afterward. If you will believe me, she went and knocked at the study door before she gave herself time to think, and when a gruff voice called out, "come in!" she did go in, right up to Mr. Laurence, who looked quite taken aback, and held out her hand, saying, with only a small tremble in her voice, "I came to thank you, sir, for—"

But she didn't finish, for he looked so friendly that she forgot her speech and, only remembering

ASTONISH (uh <u>stahn</u> ish) *v.* **-ing**, **-ed**
    to amaze or astound
        Synonyms: surprise, shock

CONFIDING (kun <u>fy</u> ding) *adj.*
    able to trust others with personal things
        Synonym: open

VANISH (<u>van</u> ish) *v.* **-ing**, **-ed**
    to leave quickly and completely
        Synonyms: disappear, fade, evaporate

that he had lost the little girl he loved, she put both arms round his neck and kissed him.

If the roof of the house had suddenly flown off, the old gentleman wouldn't have been more **astonished**. But he liked it. Oh, dear, yes, he liked it amazingly! And he was so touched and pleased by that **confiding** little kiss that all his scariness **vanished**, and he just set her on his knee, and laid his wrinkled cheek against her rosy one, feeling as if he had got his own little granddaughter back again.

CONDESCENSION (kon di <u>sen</u> shun) *n.*
self-importance in conversation and action
Synonyms: disdain, arrogance

CHAPTER 6

On a chilly September day, Jo bounced in, laid herself on the sofa, and affected to read the local newspaper.

"Have you anything interesting there?" asked Meg, with **condescension**.

"Nothing but a story. Won't amount to much, I guess," returned Jo, carefully keeping the name of the paper out of sight.

"You'd better read it aloud. That will amuse us and keep you out of mischief," said Amy in her most grown-up tone.

PATHETIC (puh <u>thet</u> ik) *adj.*
　causing sadness and pity
　　Synonyms: pitiable, tragic

APPROVING (uh <u>proov</u> ing) *adj.*
　having a good opinion of something
　　Synonyms: praising, supporting,
　　commending

TRAGIC (<u>traj</u> ik) *adj.*
　disastrous and unfortunate
　　Synonyms: sad, awful

COUNTENANCE (<u>kown</u> tuh nence) *n.*
　the expression on someone's face
　　Synonyms: face, look

SOLEMNITY (suh <u>lem</u> nuh tee) *n.*
　a state of seriousness
　　Synonyms: gravity, earnestness

"What's the name?" asked Beth, wondering why Jo kept her face behind the sheet.

"The Rival Painters."

"That sounds good. Read it," said Meg.

With a loud "Hem!" and a long breath, Jo began to read very fast. The girls listened with interest, for the tale was romantic and somewhat **pathetic**, as most of the characters died in the end. "I like that part about the splendid picture," was Amy's **approving** remark, as Jo paused.

"I prefer the lovering part. Viola and Angelo are two of our favorite names, isn't that queer?" said Meg, wiping her eyes, for the part about the lovers was **tragic**.

"Who wrote it?" asked Beth, who had caught a glimpse of Jo's face.

The reader suddenly sat up, cast away the paper, displaying a flushed **countenance**, and with a funny mixture of **solemnity** and excitement replied in a loud voice, "Your sister."

"You?" cried Meg, dropping her work.

"It's very good," said Amy critically.

"I knew it! I knew it! Oh, my Jo, I am so

EXULT (eks <u>ult</u>) *v.* **-ing**, **-ed**
to be very happy or excited
Synonyms: revel, gloat

GRACIOUSLY (<u>gray</u> shuss lee) *adv.*
done with tact and kindness
Synonyms: politely, amiably

AFFECTIONATE (uh <u>fek</u> shuh nuht) *adj.*
caring and loving
Synonyms: warm, open

JUBILEE (<u>joo</u> buh lee) *n.*
a big party or celebration
Synonyms: event, festival

proud!" and Beth ran to hug her sister and **exult** over this splendid success.

Dear me, how delighted they all were, to be sure! How Meg wouldn't believe it till she saw the words "Miss Josephine March" actually printed in the paper. How **graciously** Amy criticized the artistic parts of the story and offered hints for a sequel, which unfortunately couldn't be carried out, as the hero and heroine were dead. How Beth got excited and skipped and sang with joy. How Hannah came in to exclaim, "Sakes alive, well I never!" in great astonishment at "that Jo's doings." How proud Mrs. March was when she knew it. How Jo laughed, with tears in her eyes, as she declared she might as well be a peacock and be done with it.

"Tell us about it." "When did it come?" "How much did you get for it?" "What will Father say?" "Won't Laurie laugh?" cried the family, all in one breath as they clustered about Jo, for these foolish, **affectionate** people made a **jubilee** of every little household joy.

"Stop jabbering, girls, and I'll tell you

DISPOSE (diss <u>pohz</u>) *v.* **-ing**, **-ed**
to get rid of or throw away
Synonyms: give, discard

everything," said Jo. Having told how she **disposed** of her tales, Jo added, "And when I went to get my answer, the man said he liked them both but didn't pay beginners. He only let them print in his paper and gave the names of the stories and their authors. It was good practice, he said, and when the beginners improved, others would pay.

"So I let him have the two stories, and today this was sent to me, and Laurie caught me with it and insisted on seeing it, so I let him. And he said it was good, and I shall write more, and he's going to get the next paid for, and I am so happy, for in time I may be able to support myself and help you all."

Jo's breath gave out here, and wrapping her head in the paper, she added to her little story with a few natural tears, for to be independent and earn the praise of those she loved were the dearest wishes of her heart, and this seemed to be the first step toward that happy end.

DESPONDENT (di <u>spon</u> duhnt) *adj.*
depressed
Synonyms: unhappy, dejected

CHAPTER 7

"November is the most disagreeable month in the whole year," said Margaret, standing at the window one dull afternoon, looking out at the frostbitten garden.

"That's the reason I was born in it," observed Jo.

Jo groaned and leaned both elbows on the table in a **despondent** attitude, but Amy chattered away energetically, and Beth, who sat at the other window, said, smiling, "Two pleasant things are going to happen right away. Marmee is coming

PERSUASIVE (pur <u>sway</u> siv) *adj.*
able to convince people easily
Synonyms: credible, influential

down the street, and Laurie is tramping through the garden as if he had something nice to tell."

In they both came, Mrs. March with her usual question, "Any letter from Father, girls?" and Laurie to say in his **persuasive** way, "Won't some of you come for a drive? I've been working away at mathematics till my head is in a muddle, and I'm going to freshen my wits by a brisk turn. It's a dull day, but the air isn't bad, and I'm going to take Brooke home, so it will be gay inside, if it isn't out. Come, Jo, you and Beth will go, won't you?"

"Of course we will."

"Much obliged, but I'm busy." And Meg whisked out her workbasket, for she had agreed with her mother that it was best, for her at least, not to drive too often with the young gentleman.

"We three will be ready in a minute," cried Amy, running away to wash her hands.

"Can I do anything for you, Madam Mother?" asked Laurie, leaning over Mrs. March's chair with the affectionate look and tone he always gave her.

"No, thank you, except call at the post office, if you'll be so kind, dear. It's our day for a letter, and

INTERRUPT (in tuh <u>ruhpt</u>) *v.* **-ing**, **-ed**
to stop something that is happening
Synonyms: disrupt, halt, disturb

HORRID (<u>hor</u> id) *adj.*
terrible or nasty
Synonyms: unpleasant, vile

EXPLODE (ek <u>splode</u>) *v.* **-ing**, **-ed**
to blow apart, usually with a loud noise
Synonyms: blast, detonate

the postman hasn't been. Father is as regular as the sun, but there's some delay on the way, perhaps."

A sharp ring **interrupted** her, and a minute after Hannah came in with a letter.

"It's one of them **horrid** <u>telegraph</u> things, mum," she said, handling it as if she was afraid it would **explode** and do some damage.

At the word "telegraph," Mrs. March snatched it, read the two lines it contained, and dropped back into her chair as white as if the little paper had sent a bullet to her heart. Laurie dashed downstairs for water, while Meg and Hannah supported her, and Jo read it aloud in a frightened voice:

Mrs. March:
Your husband is very ill. Come at once.

S. HALE
Blank Hospital, Washington.

How still the room was as they listened breathlessly, how strangely the day darkened outside, and how suddenly the whole world seemed to change, as the girls gathered about their mother, feeling as if all the happiness and support of their lives was about to be taken from them.

HEARTILY (<u>har</u> tuh lee) *adv.*
  done with much enthusiasm
    Synonyms: energetically, passionately

PRESENTLY (<u>prez</u> uhnt lee) *adv.*
  1. without much delay, quickly
    Synonyms: shortly, soon
  2. immediately, at that time
    Synonyms: now, currently

Mrs. March was herself again soon, read the message over, and stretched out her arms to her daughters, saying, in a tone they never forgot, "I shall go at once, but it may be too late. Oh, children, children, help me to bear it!"

For several minutes there was nothing but the sound of sobbing in the room, mingled with broken words of comfort.

"The Lord keep the dear man! I won't waste no time a-cryin', but I'll git your things ready right away, mum," Hannah said **heartily**, as she wiped her face on her apron, gave her mistress a warm shake of the hand with her own hard one, and went away to work like three women in one.

"She's right, there's no time for tears now. Be composed, girls, and let me think." They tried to be calm, poor things, as their mother sat up, looking pale but steady, and put away her grief to think and plan for them.

"Where's Laurie?" she asked **presently**, when she had collected her thoughts and decided on the first duties to be done.

"Here, ma'am. Oh, let me do something!"

SACRED (<u>say</u> krid) *adj.*
1. important, greatly respected
   Synonyms: revered, holy
2. personal
   Synonym: private

EXCURSION (ek <u>skur</u> zhuhn) *n.*
a journey
   Synonyms: trip, outing, expedition

EQUIPPED (i <u>kwipt</u>) *adj.*
having the right materials
   Synonyms: ready, prepared

cried the boy, hurrying from the next room whither he had withdrawn, feeling that their first sorrow was too **sacred** for even his friendly eyes to see.

"Send a telegram saying I will come at once. The next train is early in the morning. I'll take that."

"What else? The horses are ready. I can go anywhere, do anything," he said, looking ready to fly to the ends of the earth.

"Leave a note at Aunt March's. Jo, give me that pen and paper."

Tearing off the blank side of one of her newly copied pages, Jo drew the table before her mother, well knowing that money for the long, sad **excursion** must be borrowed, and feeling as if she would do anything to add a little to the sum for her father.

"Now go, dear, but don't kill yourself driving at a pace. There is no need of that."

Mrs. March's warning was evidently thrown away, for five minutes later Laurie tore by the window on his own speedy horse, riding as if for his life.

"Jo, run and tell Mrs. King that I can't come visit today. On the way get these things. I'll put them down, they'll be needed, and I must go **equipped**

INVALID (<u>in</u> vuh lid) *n.*
someone who is ill or injured
Synonym: patient

PERTURBED (pur <u>turbd</u>) *adj.*
troubled or anxious
Synonyms: nervous, agitated

for nursing. Hospital stores are not always good. Beth, go and ask Mr. Laurence for a couple of bottles of old wine. I'm not too proud to beg for Father. He shall have the best of everything. Amy, tell Hannah to get down the black trunk, and Meg, come and help me find my things, for I'm half bewildered."

Writing, thinking, and directing all at once might well bewilder the poor lady, and Meg begged her to sit quietly in her room for a little while and let them work. Everyone scattered like leaves before a gust of wind, and the quiet, happy household was broken up as suddenly as if the paper had been an evil spell.

Mr. Laurence came hurrying back with Beth, bringing every comfort the kind old gentleman could think of for the **invalid** and friendliest promises of protection for the girls during the mother's absence, which comforted her very much. Laurie's tutor, Mr. Brooke, suddenly came forward.

"I'm very sorry to hear of this, Miss March," he said to Meg, in a kind, quiet tone, which sounded very pleasant to her **perturbed** spirit.

COMMISSIONS (kuh <u>mish</u> uhns) *n.*
  jobs or tasks
    Synonyms: errands, duties

EARNESTLY (<u>ur</u> nist lee) *adv.*
  eagerly yet seriously
    Synonyms: intently, industriously

"I came to offer myself as escort to your mother. Mr. Laurence has **commissions** for me in Washington, and it will give me real satisfaction to be of service to her there."

Down dropped the boots Meg was holding, and the tea she was making nearly followed, as Meg put out her hand, with a face so full of gratitude that Mr. Brooke would have felt repaid for a much greater sacrifice than the one of time and comfort which he was about to take.

"How kind you all are! Mother will accept, I'm sure, and it will be such a relief to know that she has someone to take care of her. Thank you very, very much!"

Meg spoke **earnestly** and forgot herself entirely till something in the brown eyes looking down at her made her remember the cooling tea. She led the way into the parlor, saying she would call her mother.

Everything was arranged by the time Laurie returned with a note from Aunt March, enclosing the desired sum with a few lines repeating what she had often said before, that she had always told

ABSURD (ab <u>surd</u>) *adj.*
silly, strange
Synonyms: ridiculous, bizarre

PREDICT (pruh <u>dikt</u>) *v.* **-ing**, **-ed**
to say what will happen in the future
Synonyms: guess, speculate

PREPARATION (preh puh <u>ray</u> shun) *n.*
something done to get ready for something
Synonyms: plan, arrangement

CONTRIBUTION (kuhn trib <u>yoo</u> shun) *n.*
gift or help given to others
Synonyms: donation, charity

them it was **absurd** for March to go into the army, had always **predicted** that no good would come of it, and she hoped they would take her advice the next time. Mrs. March put the note in the fire, the money in her purse, and went on with her **preparations**, with her lips folded tightly in a way which Jo would have understood if she had been there.

The short afternoon wore away. All other errands were done, and Meg and her mother were busy at some necessary needlework, while Beth and Amy got tea, and Hannah finished her ironing with what she called a "slap and a bang," but still Jo did not come. They began to get anxious, and Laurie went off to find her, for no one knew what Jo might take into her head. He missed her, however, and she came walking in with a very queer expression of countenance, for there was a mixture of fun and fear, satisfaction and regret in it, which puzzled the family as much as did the roll of bills she laid before her mother, saying with a little choke in her voice, "That's my **contribution** toward making Father comfortable and bringing him home!"

RASH (rash) *adj.*
    done quickly and without thought
        Synonyms: hasty, reckless

ABUNDANT (uh <u>bun</u> duhnt) *adj.*
    having a great amount
        Synonyms: plentiful, profuse

INDIFFERENT (in <u>dif</u> uhr uhnt) *adj.*
    not interested or caring
        Synonyms: unconcerned, apathetic

DECEIVE (di <u>seev</u>) *v.* **-ing, -ed**
    to trick someone into believing something
        Synonym: mislead

VANITY (<u>van</u> uh tee) *n.*
    an excessive amount of concern for one's
    appearance
        Synonyms: pride, self-involvement

"My dear, where did you get it? Twenty-five dollars! Jo, I hope you haven't done anything **rash**?"

"No, it's mine honestly. I didn't beg, borrow, or steal it. I earned it, and I don't think you'll blame me, for I only sold what was my own."

As she spoke, Jo took off her bonnet, and a general outcry arose, for all her **abundant** hair was cut short.

"Your hair! Your beautiful hair!" "Oh, Jo, how could you? Your one beauty." "My dear girl, there was no need of this." "She doesn't look like my Jo any more, but I love her dearly for it!"

As everyone exclaimed and Beth hugged the cropped head tenderly, Jo assumed an **indifferent** air, which did not **deceive** anyone at all, and said, rumpling up the brown bush and trying to look as if she liked it, "It doesn't affect the fate of the nation, so don't wail, Beth. It will be good for my **vanity**, I was getting too proud of my wig. It will do my brains good to have that mop taken off. My head feels deliciously light and cool, and the barber said I could soon have a curly crop, which will

SACRIFICE (<u>sak</u> ruh fyss) *v.* **-ing**, **-ed**
to give up something important
Synonyms: forfeit, surrender

CONDEMNED (kuhn <u>demd</u>) *adj.*
strongly disapproved of
Synonyms: denounced, rebuked

SALARY (<u>sal</u> uh ree) *n.*
the amount of money someone gets from a job
Synonyms: pay, wages

be boyish, becoming, and easy to keep in order. I'm satisfied, so please take the money and let's have supper."

"Tell me all about it, Jo. I am not quite satisfied, but I can't blame you, for I know how willingly you **sacrificed** your vanity, as you call it, to your love. But, my dear, it was not necessary, and I'm afraid you will regret it one of these days," said Mrs. March.

"No, I won't!" returned Jo stoutly, feeling much relieved that her prank was not entirely **condemned**.

"What made you do it?" asked Amy, who would as soon have thought of cutting off her head as her pretty hair.

"Well, I was wild to do something for Father," replied Jo, as they gathered about the table, for healthy young people can eat even in the midst of trouble. "I hate to borrow as much as Mother does, and I knew Aunt March would croak, she always does, even if you only ask for a few cents. Meg gave all her **salary** toward the rent, and I got some clothes with mine, so I felt wicked, and was bound

EARNINGS (<u>urn</u> engs) *n.*
payments for work
Synonyms: income, pay

AWE (aw) *n.*
a feeling of great respect
Synonyms: wonder, admiration

to have some money, even if I sold the nose off my face to get it."

"You needn't feel wicked, my child! You had no winter things and got the simplest with your own hard **earnings**," said Mrs. March with a look that warmed Jo's heart.

"I hadn't the least idea of selling my hair at first, but as I went along I kept thinking what I could do, and feeling as if I'd like to dive into some of the rich stores and help myself. In a barber's window I saw tails of hair with the prices marked, and one black tail, not so thick as mine, was forty dollars. It came to me all of a sudden that I had one thing to make money out of, and without stopping to think, I walked in to ask if they bought hair and what they would give for mine."

"I don't see how you dared to do it," said Beth in a tone of **awe**.

"Oh, he was a little man who looked as if he merely lived to oil his hair. He rather stared at first, as if he wasn't used to having girls bounce into his shop and ask him to buy their hair. He said he didn't care about mine, it wasn't the fashionable

DIVERT (dy <u>vurt</u>) *v.* **-ing**, **-ed**
  to remove someone's attention from something
    Synonyms: redirect, reroute

CONFESS (kuhn <u>fess</u>) *v.* **-ing**, **-ed**
  to admit to wrongdoing
    Synonyms: acknowledge, own up to

color, and he never paid much for it in the first place. The work put into it made it dear, and so on. It was getting late, and I was afraid if it wasn't done right away that I shouldn't have it done at all, and you know when I start to do a thing, I hate to give it up. So I begged him to take it, and told him why I was in such a hurry. It was silly, I dare say, but it changed his mind, for I got rather excited, and told the story in my topsy-turvy way, and his wife heard, and said so kindly, 'Take it, Thomas, and oblige the young lady. I'd do as much for our Jimmy any day if I had a lock of hair worth selling."

"Who was Jimmy?" asked Amy, who liked to have things explained as they went along.

"Her son, she said, who was in the army. How friendly such things make strangers feel, don't they? She talked away all the time the man clipped, and **diverted** my mind nicely."

"Didn't you feel dreadfully when the first cut came?" asked Meg, with a shiver.

"I took a last look at my hair while the man got his things, and that was the end of it. I never worry over trifles like that. I will **confess**, though, I

PROSPECT (<u>pross</u> pekt) *n.*
the hope that something will happen
Synonyms: possibility, expectation

CONSOLER (kuhn <u>sole</u> ur) *n.*
someone or something who provides comfort
during a time of difficulty
Synonyms: soother, mediator

felt odd when I saw the dear old hair laid out on the table, and felt only the short rough ends on my head. It almost seemed as if I'd an arm or leg off. The woman saw me look at it, and picked out a long lock for me to keep. I'll give it to you, Marmee, just to remember past glories by, for short hair is so comfortable I don't think I shall ever have a mane again."

Mrs. March folded the wavy chestnut lock, and laid it away with a short gray one in her desk. She only said, "Thank you, deary," but something in her face made the girls change the subject, and talk as cheerfully as they could about Mr. Brooke's kindness, the **prospect** of a fine day tomorrow, and the happy times they would have when Father came home to be nursed.

No one wanted to go to bed when at ten o'clock Mrs. March put away the last finished job, and said, "Come girls." Beth went to the piano and played their father's favorite song. All began bravely, but broke down one by one till Beth was left alone, singing with all her heart, for to her music was always a sweet **consoler**.

BUSIED (<u>biz</u> eed) *adj.*
engaged in activities
Synonym: active

PROTECTION (pruh <u>tek</u> shun) *n.*
someone or something that keeps one safe
Synonyms: defense, shelter

CHAPTER 8

The next morning nobody talked much. But as the time drew very near and they sat waiting for the carriage, Mrs. March said to the girls, who were all **busied** about her, one folding her shawl, another smoothing out the strings of her bonnet, a third putting on her overshoes, and a fourth fastening up her traveling bag, "Children, I leave you to Hannah's care and Mr. Laurence's **protection**. Hannah is faithfulness itself, and our good neighbor will guard you as if you were his own. I have no fears for you, yet I am anxious

GRIEVE (greev) *v.* **-ing**, **-ed**
> to feel sad, usually because of death or loss
>> Synonyms: mourn, lament

SOLACE (<u>sahl</u> iss) *n.*
> relief from pain or unhappiness
>> Synonyms: consolation, comfort

PRUDENT (<u>prood</u> uhnt) *adj.*
> thinking things out carefully and thoughtfully
>> Synonyms: cautious, sensible

PERPLEXITY (pur <u>pleks</u> uh tee) *n.*
> something that is strange or unclear
>> Synonyms: mystification, puzzlement

OBEDIENT (oh <u>bee</u> dee uhnt) *adj.*
> following instructions
>> Synonyms: compliant, submissive

that you should take this trouble rightly. Don't **grieve** and fret when I am gone or think that you can be idle and comfort yourselves by being idle and trying to forget. Go on with your work as usual, for work is a blessed **solace**. Hope and keep busy, and whatever happens, remember that you never can be fatherless."

"Yes, Mother."

"Meg, dear, be **prudent**, watch over your sisters, consult Hannah, and in any **perplexity**, go to Mr. Laurence. Be patient, Jo, don't get despondent or do rash things, write to me often, and be my brave girl, ready to help and cheer all. Beth, comfort yourself with your music, and be faithful to the little home duties, and you, Amy, help all you can, be **obedient**, and keep happy safe at home."

"We will, Mother! We will!"

Laurie and his grandfather came over to see her off, and Mr. Brooke looked so strong and sensible and kind that the girls named him "Mr. Greatheart" on the spot.

"Goodbye, my darlings! God bless and keep us all!" whispered Mrs. March, as she kissed

OMEN (<u>oh</u> muhn) *n.*
a sign that indicates the future
Synonyms: forecast, prophesy

DEVOTED (div <u>voh</u> ted) *adj.*
showing great commitment and affection
Synonyms: loyal, dedicated

SYMPATHY (<u>sim</u> puh thee) *n.*
understanding and caring about another
Synonyms: pity, compassion

INFECTIOUSLY (in <u>fek</u> shuhss lee) *adv.*
spreading quickly and easily
Synonym: contagiously

FORLORNLY (fore <u>lorn</u> lee) *adv.*
in a sad way
Synonyms: unhappily, miserably

one dear little face after the other and hurried into the carriage.

As she rolled away, the sun came out, and looking back, she saw it shining on the group at the gate like a good **omen**. They saw it also and smiled and waved their hands, and the last thing she beheld as she turned the corner was the four bright faces, and behind them like bodyguards, old Mr. Laurence, faithful Hannah, and **devoted** Laurie.

"How kind everyone is to us!" she said, turning to find fresh proof of it in the respectful **sympathy** of the young man's face.

"I don't see how they can help it," returned Mr. Brooke, laughing so **infectiously** that Mrs. March could not help smiling. And so the journey began with sunshine, smiles, and cheerful words.

"I feel as if there had been an earthquake," said Jo, as their neighbors went home to breakfast, leaving them to rest and refresh themselves.

"It seems as if half the house was gone," added Meg **forlornly**.

Beth opened her lips to say something, but could only point to the pile of nicely mended <u>hose</u>

BITTERLY (<u>bit</u> ur lee) *adv.*
in an upset or miserable way
Synonyms: sadly, unhappily

DILIGENTLY (<u>dil</u> uh juhnt lee) *adv.*
done with much work and effort
Synonyms: thoroughly, attentively

which lay on Mother's table, showing that even in her last hurried moments she had thought and worked for them. It was a little thing, but it went straight to their hearts, and in spite of their brave resolutions, they all broke down and cried **bitterly**.

The girls worked **diligently** to forget their troubles. Hard weeks passed, but news from their father comforted the girls very much, for though dangerously ill, the presence of the best and tenderest of nurses had already done him good. He seemed much improved, and everyone was relieved. Their parents were soon to return home.

DEPICT (di <u>pikt</u>) *v.* **-ing**, **-ed**
  to show something using words or pictures
  Synonyms: describe, portray

CHAPTER 9

I don't think I have any words in which to describe the meeting of the mother and daughters when Mrs. March finally made her way back home. Such hours are beautiful to live but very hard to **depict**, so I will leave it to the imagination of my readers, merely saying that the house was full of genuine happiness, for they all woke to see their mother's face.

Hannah had "dished up" an astonishing breakfast for the traveler, finding it impossible to vent her excitement in any other way, and Meg and Jo fed their mother like dutiful young storks, while

FATIGUE (fuh <u>teeg</u>) *n.*
extreme tiredness
Synonyms: weakness, exhaustion

GESTURE (<u>jess</u> chur) *n.*
an action that shows feeling
Synonyms: signal, motion

they listened to her whispered account of Father's state, Mr. Brooke's promise to stay and nurse him, the delays which a storm occasioned on the homeward journey, and the unspeakable comfort Laurie's hopeful face had given her when she arrived, worn out with **fatigue**, anxiety, and cold.

That evening while Meg was writing to her father to report the traveler's safe arrival, Jo slipped upstairs into Beth's room, and finding her mother sitting there, stood a minute twisting her fingers in her hair, with a worried **gesture** and an undecided look.

"What is it, deary?" asked Mrs. March, with a face which invited confidence.

"I want to tell you something, Mother."

"About Meg?"

"How quickly you guessed! Yes, it's about her, and though it's a little thing, it fidgets me."

"Beth is asleep. Speak low, and tell me all about it. That Moffat boy who wants to take her away and marry her hasn't been here, I hope?" asked Mrs. March rather sharply.

"No. I should have shut the door in his face

CONTEMPT (kuhn <u>tempt</u>) *n.*
a lack of respect
Synonyms: disdain, scorn

BLUSH (blush) *v.* **-ing**, **-ed**
to turn red from embarrassment
Synonyms: flush, redden

SENSIBLE (<u>sen</u> suh buhl) *adj.*
reasonable
Synonyms: rational, careful

if he had," said Jo, settling herself on the floor at her mother's feet. "Last summer Meg left a pair of gloves over at the Laurences' and only one was returned. We forgot about it, till Laurie told me that Mr. Brooke owned that he liked Meg but didn't dare say so, she was so young and he, so poor. Now, isn't it a dreadful condition of things?"

"Do you think Meg cares for him?" asked Mrs. March, with an anxious look.

"Mercy me! I don't know anything about love and such nonsense!" cried Jo, with a funny mixture of interest and **contempt**. "In novels, the girls show it by starting and **blushing**, fainting away, growing thin, and acting like fools. Now Meg does not do anything of the sort. She eats and drinks and sleeps like a **sensible** creature, she looks straight in my face when I talk about that man, and only blushes a little bit when Laurie jokes about lovers. I forbid him to do it, but he doesn't mind me as he ought."

"Then you fancy that Meg is not interested in John?"

"Who?" cried Jo, staring.

WRATHFUL (<u>rath</u> fuhl) *adj.*
　violently angry
　　Synonyms: furious, irate

EXCELLENT (<u>ek</u> suh luhnt) *adj.*
　of the highest quality
　　Synonyms: outstanding, brilliant

DISCONSOLATE (diss <u>cahn</u> suh luht) *adj.*
　unhappy, beyond cheering up
　　Synonyms: dreary, dejected, miserable

REPREHENSIBLE (rep ree <u>henss</u> uh buhl) *adj.*
　unacceptable, at fault
　　Synonyms: liable, culpable

"Mr. Brooke. I call him 'John' now. We fell into the way of doing so at the hospital, and he likes it."

"Oh, dear! I know you'll take his part. He's been good to Father, and you won't send him away, but let Meg marry him, if she wants to. Mean thing! To go petting Papa and helping you, just to force you into liking him." And Jo pulled her hair again with a **wrathful** tweak.

"My dear, don't get angry about it, and I will tell you how it happened. John went with me at Mr. Laurence's request and was so good to poor Father that we couldn't help getting fond of him. He was perfectly open and honorable about Meg, for he told us he loved her but would earn a comfortable home before he asked her to marry him. He is a truly **excellent** young man, and we could not refuse to listen to him. But I will not consent to Meg's engaging herself so young."

Jo leaned her chin on her knees in a **disconsolate** attitude and shook her fist at the **reprehensible** John. Mrs. March sighed, and Jo looked up with an air of relief.

"You don't like it, Mother? I'm glad of it.

CONSCIENTIOUS (kon shee <u>en</u> shuss) *adj.*
careful and correct
Synonyms: thorough, meticulous

FALTER (<u>fawl</u> tur) *v.* **-ing**, **-ed**
to become unsure and inconsistent
Synonyms: hesitate, waver

POSSESSION (puh <u>zesh</u> uhn) *n.*
something one owns or has
Synonym: ownership

Let's send him about his business and not tell Meg a word of it but all be happy together as we always have been."

"Your father and I have agreed that she shall not bind herself in any way, nor be married, before twenty. If she and John love one another, they can wait and test the love by doing so. She is **conscientious**, and I have no fear of her treating him unkindly. My pretty, tenderhearted girl! I hope things will go happily with her."

"Hadn't you rather have her marry a rich man?" asked Jo, as her mother's voice **faltered** a little over the last words.

"Money is a good and useful thing, Jo, and I hope my girls will never feel the need of it too bitterly nor be tempted by too much. I should like to know that John was firmly established in some good business, which gave him an income large enough to keep free from debt and make Meg comfortable. I am content to see Meg begin humbly, for if I am not mistaken she will be rich in the **possession** of a good man's heart, and that is better than a fortune."

"I understand, Mother, and quite agree, but

GENEROUS (<u>jen</u> ur uhss) *adj.*
giving and caring with time and money
Synonyms: munificent, charitable

SECURELY (si <u>kyoor</u> lee) *adv.*
done without risk
Synonym: safely

I'm disappointed about Meg, for I'd planned to have her marry Laurie by-and-by and sit in the lap of luxury all her days. Wouldn't it be nice?" asked Jo, looking up with a brighter face.

"He is younger than she, you know," began Mrs. March, but Jo broke in:

"Only a little. He's old for his age and tall and can be quite grown-up in his manners if he likes. Then he's rich and **generous** and good and loves us all, and I say it's a pity my plan is spoiled."

"I'm afraid Laurie is hardly grown-up enough for Meg and altogether too much of a weathercock just now for anyone to depend on. Don't make plans, Jo, but let time and their own hearts mate your friends. We can't meddle **securely** in such matters and had better not get 'romantic rubbish,' as you call it, into our heads lest it spoil our friendship."

"Well, I won't, but I hate to see things going all crisscross and getting snarled up when a pull here and a snip there would straighten it out. I wish wearing flatirons on our heads would keep us from growing up. But buds will be roses, and kittens cats, more's the pity!"

INEXPRESSIBLY (in eks <u>press</u> uh blee) *adj.*
in a way that cannot be put into words
Synonyms: indescribably, deeply

"What's that about flatirons and cats?" asked Meg, as she crept into the room with the finished letter to Mr. March in her hand.

"Only one of my stupid speeches. I'm going to bed," said Jo, unfolding herself like an animated puzzle.

"Quite right and beautifully written. Please add that I send my love to John," said Mrs. March, as she glanced over the letter and gave it back.

"Do you call him 'John'?" asked Meg, smiling, with her innocent eyes looking down into her mother's.

"Yes, he has been like a son to us, and we are very fond of him," replied Mrs. March, returning the look with a keen one.

"I'm glad of that. He is so lonely. Good night, Mother, dear. It is so **inexpressibly** comfortable to have you here," was Meg's answer.

The kiss her mother gave her was a very tender one, and as she went away, Mrs. March said, with a mixture of satisfaction and regret, "She does not love John yet but will soon learn to."

PATRONIZING (<u>pat</u> ruh nyz ing) *adj.*
  acting as if one is better than someone else
  Synonym: condescending

AGGRAVATE (<u>ag</u> ruh vate) *v.* **-ing**, **-ed**
  1. to irritate
  Synonym: annoy
  2. to make something worse
  Synonyms: worsen, exacerbate

DIGNIFIED (<u>dig</u> nuh fyd) *adj.*
  noble and composed
  Synonyms: grand, distinguished

CHAPTER 10

Jo's face was a study the next day for the secret rather weighed upon her, and she found it hard not to look mysterious and important. Meg observed it but did not trouble herself to make inquiries, for she had learned that the best way to manage Jo was by the law of opposites, so she felt sure of being told everything if she did not ask. She was rather surprised, therefore, when the silence remained unbroken, and Jo assumed a **patronizing** air, which decidedly **aggravated** Meg, who in turn assumed an air of **dignified** reserve and devoted

INCORRIGIBLE (in <u>kor</u> ij uh buhl) *adj.*
impossible to control or correct
Synonyms: hopeless, persistent

PERSEVERANCE (pur suh <u>veer</u> uhnss) *n.*
a continued action or belief
Synonyms: firmness, resolve

INDIGNANT (in <u>dig</u> nuhnt) *adj.*
being upset or annoyed because of unfairness
Synonyms: offended, resentful

RETALIATION (ri <u>tal</u> ee ay shun) *n.*
revenge
Synonyms: reprisal, retribution

herself to her mother. This left Jo to her own devices, and Laurie became her only refuge. But, much as she enjoyed his society, she rather dreaded him just then, for he was an **incorrigible** tease, and she feared he would coax the secret from her.

She was quite right, for the mischief-loving lad no sooner suspected a mystery than he set himself to find it out and led Jo a trying life of it. He bribed, ridiculed, threatened, and scolded; he tried to surprise the truth from her; he declared he knew, then that he didn't care; and at last, by dint of **perseverance**, he satisfied himself that it concerned Meg and Mr. Brooke. Feeling **indignant** that he was not taken into his tutor's confidence, he set his wits to work to devise some proper **retaliation** for the slight.

Meg meanwhile was absorbed in preparations for her father's return. But all of a sudden a change seemed to come over her, and, for a day or two, she was quite unlike herself. She started when spoken to, blushed when looked at, was very quiet, and sat over her sewing with a timid, troubled look on her face. To her mother's inquiries she answered

TOLERANT (<u>tahl</u> ur uhnt) *adj.*
accepting the views of others
Synonyms: liberal, open-minded

DISTRIBUTE (diss <u>trib</u> yoot) *v.* **-ing**, **-ed**
to deliver or pass things out
Synonyms: dole, allocate

that she was quite well, and Jo's she silenced by begging to be let alone.

"She feels it in the air – love, I mean – and she's going very fast. She's got most of the symptoms – is twittery and cross, doesn't eat, lies awake, and mopes in corners. I caught her singing a song he gave her. And once she said 'John,' as you do, and then turned as red as a poppy. Whatever shall we do?" said Jo, looking ready for any measures.

"Nothing but wait. Let her alone, be kind and **tolerant**, and Father's coming will settle everything," replied her mother.

"Here's a note to you, Meg, all sealed up. How odd! Laurie never seals mine," said Jo next day, as she **distributed** the contents of the little post office.

Mrs. March and Jo were deep in their own affairs when a sound from Meg made them look up to see her staring at her note with a frightened face.

"My child, what is it?" cried her mother, running to her, while Jo tried to take the paper which had done the mischief.

REPROACHFULLY (ri <u>prohch</u> fuh lee) *adv.*
placing blame
Synonyms: accusingly, reprovingly

PECULIAR (pi <u>kyoo</u> lyur) *adj.*
odd or irregular
Synonyms: weird, queer

RESTRAIN (ri <u>strayn</u>) *v.* **-ing**, **-ed**
to prevent, hold back
Synonyms: contain, control

PASSION (<u>pash</u> uhn) *n.*
a strong love or enthusiasm
Synonyms: obsession, fervor

"It's all a mistake, he didn't send it. Oh, Jo, how could you do it?" and Meg hid her face in her hands, crying as if her heart were quite broken.

"Me! I've done nothing! What's she talking about?" cried Jo, bewildered.

Meg's mild eyes kindled with anger as she pulled a crumpled note from her pocket and threw it at Jo, saying **reproachfully**, "You wrote it, and that bad boy helped you. How could you be so rude, so mean, and cruel to us both?"

Jo hardly heard her, for she and her mother were reading the note, which was written in a **peculiar** hand.

My Dearest Margaret,

I can no longer **restrain** my **passion** and must know my fate before I return. I dare not tell your parents yet, but I think they would consent if they knew that we adored one another. Mr. Laurence will help me to some good place, and then, my sweet girl, you will make me happy. I implore you to say nothing to your family yet, but to send one word of hope through Laurie to

Your devoted John.

"Oh, the little villain! Laurie had to have

EXECUTE (<u>ek</u> suh kyoot) *v.* **-ing**, **-ed**
to perform an action
Synonyms: implement, carry out

done this to help Mr. Brooke's cause. I'll give him a hearty scolding and bring him over to beg pardon," cried Jo, burning to **execute** immediate justice.

Her mother held her back, saying, with a look she seldom wore, "Stop, Jo, you must clear yourself first. You have played so many pranks that I am afraid you have had a hand in this."

"On my word, Mother, I haven't! I never saw that note before, and I don't know anything about it, as true as I live!" said Jo, so earnestly that they believed her. "If I had taken part in it I'd have done it better than this and have written a sensible note. I should think you'd have known Mr. Brooke wouldn't write such stuff as that," she added, scornfully tossing down the paper.

"It's like his writing," faltered Meg, comparing it with the note in her hand.

"Oh, Meg, you didn't answer it?" cried Mrs. March quickly.

"Yes, I did!" and Meg hid her face again, overcome with shame.

"Here's a scrape! Do let me bring that

LECTURE (<u>lek</u> chur) *v.* **-ing**, **-ed**
to reprimand or criticize through a speech
Synonyms: scold, harangue

APPREHENSIVE (ap ri <u>hen</u> siv) *adj.*
scared and worried
Synonyms: anxious, uneasy

wicked boy over to explain and be **lectured**. I can't rest till I get hold of him." And Jo made for the door again.

"Hush! Let me handle this, for it is worse than I thought. Margaret, tell me the whole story," commanded Mrs. March, sitting down by Meg, yet keeping hold of Jo, lest she should fly off.

"I received the first letter from Laurie, who didn't look as if he knew anything about it," began Meg, without looking up. "I was **apprehensive** at first and meant to tell you. Then I remembered how you liked Mr. Brooke, so I thought you wouldn't mind if I kept my little secret for a few days. I'm so silly that I liked to think no one knew, and while I was deciding what to say, I felt like the girls in books, who have such things to do. Forgive me, Mother, I'm paid for my silliness now. I never can look him in the face again."

"What did you say to him?" asked Mrs. March.

"I only said I was too young to do anything about it yet, that I didn't wish to have secrets from you, and he must speak to Father. I was very

ROGUISH (<u>rohg</u> ish) *adj.*
wild, mischievous
Synonyms: impish, naughty

LIBERTY (<u>lib</u> ur tee) *n.*
action done without consent
Synonyms: rights, authority

MISERY (<u>miz</u> ur ee) *n.*
great unhappiness
Synonyms: sadness, depression

grateful for his kindness and would be his friend, but nothing more, for a long while."

Mrs. March smiled, as if well pleased, and Jo clapped her hands, exclaiming, with a laugh, "Tell on, Meg! What did he say to that?"

"He writes in a different way entirely, telling me that he never sent any love letter at all, and he is very sorry that my **roguish** sister, Jo, should take **liberties** with our names. It's very kind and respectful, but think how dreadful for me!"

Meg leaned against her mother, looking the image of **misery**, and Jo tramped about the room, calling Laurie names. All of a sudden she stopped, caught up the two notes, and after looking at them closely, said decidedly, "I don't believe Brooke ever saw either of these letters. Laurie wrote both and keeps yours to crow over me with because I wouldn't tell him my secret."

"Don't have any secrets, Jo. Tell it to Mother and keep out of trouble, as I should have done," said Meg warningly.

Seeing Meg's usually gentle temper was roused and her pride hurt by this mischievous

DISCRETION (diss <u>kresh</u> uhn) *n.*
the condition of saying appropriate things
Synonyms: tact, judgment

CULPRIT (<u>kuhl</u> prit) *n.*
someone guilty of a crime or misdeed
Synonym: criminal

PENITENT (<u>pen</u> uh tuhnt) *adj.*
feeling sorry for having done something bad
Synonyms: remorseful, repentant

joke, Mrs. March soothed her by promises of entire silence and great **discretion** for the future.

Meanwhile, Jo went to bring Laurie to answer for his mischief. The instant Laurie was heard in the hall, Meg fled into the study, and Mrs. March received the **culprit** alone. Jo had not told him why he was wanted, fearing he wouldn't come, but he knew the minute he saw Mrs. March's face and stood twirling his hat with a guilty air, which made him seem guilty at once. Jo was dismissed but chose to march up and down the hall, having some fear that the prisoner might bolt. The sound of voices in the parlor rose and fell for half an hour, but what happened during that interview the girls never knew.

When they were called in, Laurie was standing by their mother with such a **penitent** face that Jo forgave him on the spot, but she did not think it wise to betray the fact. Meg received his humble apology and was much comforted by the assurance that Brooke knew nothing of the joke.

"I'll never tell him to my dying day, wild horses shan't drag it out of me, so you'll forgive

MALICIOUS (muh <u>lish</u> uhss) *adj.*
mean spirited
Synonyms: hateful, spiteful

ABOMINABLE (uh <u>bom</u> uh nuh buhl) *adj.*
disgusting and terrible
Synonyms: repulsive, monstrous

DISAPPROBATION (diss uh pruh <u>bay</u> shuhn) *n.*
the condition of showing disapproval
Synonyms: condemnation, dissatisfaction

me, Meg, and I'll do anything to show how out-and-out sorry I am," he added, looking very much ashamed of himself.

"I'll try, but it was a very ungentlemanly thing to do. I didn't think you could be so sly and **malicious**, Laurie," replied Meg, trying to hide her maidenly confusion under a gravely reproachful air.

"It was altogether **abominable**, and I don't deserve to be spoken to for a month, but you will, though, won't you?"

Meg pardoned him, and Mrs. March's grave face relaxed in spite of her efforts to keep sober.

Jo stood aloof, meanwhile, trying to harden her heart against him and succeeding only in primming up her face into an expression of entire **disapprobation**. Laurie looked at her once or twice, but as she showed no sign of relenting, he felt injured and turned his back on her till the others were done with him, when he made her a low bow and walked off without a word.

As soon as he had gone, she wished she had been more forgiving, and when Meg and her

IMPULSE (<u>im</u> puhlss) *n.*
a sudden whim or action
Synonyms: desire, urge

TANTRUM (<u>tan</u> truhm) *n.*
angry outburst or expression
Synonyms: fit, explosion

mother went upstairs, she felt lonely and longed for Laurie. After resisting for some time, she yielded to the **impulse**, and armed with a book to return, went over to the big house.

"Is Mr. Laurence in?" asked Jo, of a house-maid, who was coming downstairs.

"Yes, Miss, but I don't believe he's seeable just yet."

"Why not? Is he ill?"

"La, no Miss, but he's had a scene with Mr. Laurie, who is in one of his **tantrums** about something, which vexes the old gentleman, so I dursn't go nigh him."

"Where is Laurie?"

"Shut up in his room, and he won't answer, though I've been a-tapping. I don't know what's to become of the dinner, for it's ready, and there's no one to eat it."

"I'll go and see what the matter is. I'm not afraid of either of them."

Up went Jo, and knocked smartly on the door of Laurie's little study.

"Stop that, or I'll open the door and make

CONTRITE (kuhn <u>tryt</u>) *adj.*
deeply sorry and ashamed
Synonyms: repentant, remorseful

CAVALIER (kav uh <u>leer</u>) *adj.*
arrogant and quick
Synonyms: offhand, inconsiderate

you!" called out the young gentleman in a threatening tone.

Jo immediately knocked again. The door flew open, and in she bounced before Laurie could recover from his surprise. Seeing that he really was out of temper, Jo, who knew how to manage him, assumed a **contrite** expression, and going artistically down upon her knees, said meekly, "Please forgive me for being so cross. I came to make it up and can't go away till I have."

"It's all right. Get up, and don't be a goose, Jo," was the **cavalier** reply to her statement.

"Thank you, I will. Could I ask what's the matter? You don't look exactly easy in your mind."

"I've been shaken, and I won't bear it!" growled Laurie indignantly.

"Who did it?" demanded Jo.

"Grandfather. If it had been anyone else I'd have—" And the injured youth finished his sentence by an energetic gesture of the right arm.

"Just because I wouldn't say what your mother wanted me for. I'd promised not to tell, and of course I wasn't going to break my word."

PUMMELED (<u>puhm</u> uhl) *adj.*
punched
Synonyms: beaten, pounded

"Couldn't you satisfy your grandpa in any other way?"

"No," replied Laurie, "he would have the truth, the whole truth, and nothing but the truth. I'd have told my part of the scrape, if I could without bringing Meg in. As I couldn't, I held my tongue and bore the scolding till the old gentleman collared me. Then I bolted, for fear I should forget myself."

"It wasn't nice, but he's sorry, I know, so go down and make up. I'll help you."

"Hanged if I do! I'm not going to be lectured and **pummeled** by everyone, just for a bit of a frolic. I was sorry about Meg and begged pardon like a man, but I won't do it again when I wasn't in the wrong. I'll run away if he doesn't apologize, to Washington to see Mr. Brooke."

"You will do nothing of the sort. I will go speak to your grandfather. If I can manage the young one, I can the old one," muttered Jo, as she walked away, leaving Laurie bent over a railroad map with his head propped up on both hands.

"Come in!" and Mr. Laurence's gruff voice

VEXED (veksd) *adj.*
  irritable or annoyed
    Synonyms: angry, displeased

sounded gruffer than ever, as Jo tapped at his door.

"It's only me, Sir, come to return a book," she said blandly, as she entered.

"Want any more?" asked the old gentleman, looking dismal and **vexed**, but trying not to show it.

"Yes, please, I think I'll try the second volume," returned Jo, hoping to pacify him by accepting a second dose of Boswell's famous *Life of Johnson,* as he had recommended that lively work.

"What has that boy been about? Don't try to shield him. I know he has been in mischief by the way he acted when he came home. I can't get a word from him. And when I threatened to shake the truth out of him he bolted upstairs and locked himself into his room."

"He did wrong, but we forgave him, and all promised not to say a word to anyone," began Jo reluctantly.

"That won't do. He shall not shelter himself behind a promise from you softhearted girls. If he's done anything amiss, he shall confess, beg

IRASCIBLE (i <u>rass</u> uh buhl) *adj.*
provoked easily to outbursts
Synonyms: touchy, grumpy

CONTRARY (<u>kon</u> trer ee) *adj.*
of an opposing or different view
Synonyms: divergent, dissimilar

pardon, and be punished. Out with it, Jo. I won't be kept in the dark."

"Indeed, Sir, I cannot tell. Mother forbade it. Laurie has confessed, asked pardon, and been punished quite enough. We don't keep silence to shield him, but someone else, and it will make more trouble if you interfere. Please don't. It was partly my fault, but it's all right now. So let's forget it, and talk about something pleasant."

"Hang it! Come down and give me your word that this harum-scarum boy of mine hasn't done anything ungrateful or impertinent. If he has, after all your kindness to him, I'll thrash him with my own hands."

The threat sounded awful but did not alarm Jo, for she knew the **irascible** old gentleman would never lift a finger against his grandson, whatever he might say to the **contrary**. She obediently descended and made as light of the prank as she could without betraying Meg or forgetting the truth.

"Hum . . . ha . . . well, if the boy held his tongue because he promised and not from

OBSTINACY (<u>ob</u> stuh nuh see) *n.*

the condition of being stubborn or hard-headed

Synonyms: determination, inflexibility

RESTRAINT (ri <u>straynt</u>) *n.*

1. control

Synonym: restriction

2. composure

Synonyms: command, self-possession

FORBEARING (fore <u>bayr</u> ing) *adj.*

patient, forgiving

Synonyms: tolerant, lenient

obstinacy, I'll forgive him. He's a stubborn fellow and hard to manage."

"So am I, but a kind word will govern me when all the king's horses and all the king's men couldn't," said Jo, trying to say a kind word for her friend, who seemed to get out of one scrape only to fall into another.

"You think I'm not kind to him, hey?" was the sharp answer.

"Oh, dear no, Sir. You are rather too kind sometimes, and then just a bit mean when he tries your patience. Don't you think you are?"

To her great relief and surprise, the old gentleman only threw his spectacles onto the table with a rattle and exclaimed frankly, "You're right, girl, I am! I love the boy, but he tries my patience past bearing, and I don't know how it will end, if we go on so."

"I'll tell you, he'll run away." Jo was sorry for that speech the minute it was made. She meant to warn him that Laurie would not bear much **restraint** and that she hoped he would be more **forbearing** with the lad.

IMPERIOUS (im <u>peer</u> ee uhss) *adj.*
controlling and commanding
Synonyms: authoritative, domineering

TESTINESS (<u>tess</u> tee nuhss) *n.*
crankiness and grouchiness
Synonyms: irritability, crabbiness

Mr. Laurence's ruddy face changed suddenly, and he sat down, with a troubled glance at the picture of a handsome man, which hung over his table. It was Laurie's father, who had run away in his youth and married against the **imperious** old man's will. Jo fancied he remembered and regretted the past, and she wished she had held her tongue.

"Naturally, you are correct, little girl," he said, pinching her cheeks good-humoredly. "Go and bring that boy down to his dinner, tell him it's all right, and advise him not to put on tragedy airs with his grandfather. I won't bear it."

"He won't come, Sir. He feels badly because you didn't believe him when he said he couldn't tell. I think the shaking hurt his feelings very much."

Jo tried to look pathetic but must have failed, for Mr. Laurence began to laugh, and she knew the day was won.

"I'm sorry for that and ought to thank him for not shaking me, I suppose. What the dickens does the fellow expect?" and the old gentleman looked a trifle ashamed of his own **testiness**.

"If I were you, I'd write him an apology, Sir.

AMIABLE (<u>ay</u> mee uh bul) *adj.*
nice, sociable
Synonyms: friendly, likeable

SUBMISSIVE (suhb <u>miss</u> iv) *adj.*
giving in to an authority figure
Synonyms: obedient, passive

DECOROUS (deh <u>kor</u> uhss) *adj.*
dignified and following what is appropriate
Synonyms: proper, prim

VIRTUOUS (<u>vur</u> choo uhss) *adj.*
morally correct
Synonym: honorable

He says he won't come down till he has one and talks about Washington and goes on in an absurd way. A formal apology will make him see how foolish he is, and it will bring him down quite **amiable**. Try it. He likes fun, and this way is better than talking. I'll carry it up and teach him his duty."

The note was written in the terms which one gentleman would use to another after offering some deep insult. Jo dropped a kiss on the top of Mr. Laurence's bald head and ran up to slip the apology under Laurie's door, advising him through the keyhole to be **submissive**, **decorous**, and a few other agreeable impossibilities. Finding the door locked again, she left the note to do its work. She was going quietly away when the young gentleman slid down the banisters and waited for her at the bottom, saying, with his most **virtuous** expression of countenance, "What a good fellow you are, Jo! Did you get blown up?" he added, laughing.

"No, he was pretty mild, on the whole."

"Ah! I got it all round. Even you cast me off over there, and I felt just ready to go to the deuce," he began apologetically.

DOLEFULLY (<u>dohl</u> fuhl ee) *adv.*
unhappily or sadly
Synonyms: miserably, woefully

PARTAKE (par <u>tayk</u>) *v.* **-ing**, **-ed**
to participate in
Synonyms: take, have

ALLUDE (uh <u>lood</u>) *v.* **-ing**, **-ed**
to mention or hint at something
Synonym: suggest

"Don't talk that way. Turn over a new leaf and begin again, Laurie."

"I keep turning over new leaves and spoiling them. And I make so many beginnings there never will be an end," he said **dolefully**.

"Go and eat your dinner. You'll feel better after it. Men always croak when they are hungry," and Jo whisked out at the front door after that.

"That's a 'label' on my 'sect,'" answered Laurie, quoting Amy, as he went to **partake** of humble pie dutifully with his grandfather, who was quite saintly in temper and overwhelmingly respectful in manner all the rest of the day.

Everyone thought the matter ended and the little cloud blown over, but the mischief was done, for though others forgot it, Meg remembered. She never **alluded** to a certain person. But she thought of him a good deal, dreamed dreams more than ever, and once Jo, rummaging her sister's desk for stamps, found a bit of paper scribbled over with the words, "Mrs. John Brooke," where at she groaned tragically and cast it into the fire, feeling that Laurie's prank had hastened the evil day for her.

RAPIDLY (<u>rap</u> id lee) *adv.*
speedily
Synonyms: swiftly, quickly

CHAPTER 11

Like sunshine after a storm were the peaceful
weeks which followed. Beth had been seriously ill,
but she improved **rapidly**. And in his letters, Mr.
March began to write of returning early in the new
year, soon after the Christmas holiday that had
come upon them.

Now and then, in this workaday world, things
do happen in the delightful storybook fashion, and
what a comfort it is. Half an hour after everyone
had said they were so happy they could only hold
one drop more, the drop came. Laurie opened the

SUPPRESSED (suh <u>pressd</u>) *adj.*
hidden from sight or put down
Synonyms: concealed, covered

STAMPEDE (stam <u>peed</u>) *n.*
a large rush of living things
Synonyms: charge, dash

EMBRACE (em <u>brayss</u>) *n.*
a tight, affectionate hug or grasp
Synonyms: squeeze, clasp

INCOHERENTLY (in koh <u>hir</u> uhnt) *adv.*
unclearly and illogically
Synonyms: inarticulately, nonsensically

parlor door and popped his head in very quietly. He might just as well have turned a somersault and uttered an Indian war whoop, for his face was so full of **suppressed** excitement and his voice so treacherously joyful that everyone jumped up, though he only said, in a queer, breathless voice, "Here's a Christmas present for the March family."

Before the words were well out of his mouth, he was whisked away somehow, and in his place appeared a tall man, muffled up to the eyes, leaning on the arm of another tall man, who tried to say something and couldn't. Of course there was a general **stampede**, and for several minutes everybody seemed to lose their wits, for the strangest things were done, and no one said a word.

Mr. March became invisible in the **embrace** of four pairs of loving arms. Jo disgraced herself by nearly fainting away and had to be doctored by Laurie. Mr. Brooke kissed Meg entirely by mistake, as he somewhat **incoherently** explained. And Amy, the dignified one, tumbled over a stool and never stopping to get up, hugged and cried over her father's boots in the most touching

PRECIPITATELY (pruh <u>sip</u> uh tuht lee) *adv.*
with speed or in a rushed way
Synonyms: preemptively, hastily

RETIRE (ri <u>tire</u>) *v.* **-ing**, **-ed**
to leave or go to bed
Synonyms: withdraw, retreat

REPOSE (rip <u>ohz</u>) *v.* **-ing**, **-ed**
to sleep or relax
Synonym: rest

manner. Mrs. March was the first to recover herself, and held up her hand with a warning, "Hush! Remember Beth. She needs to rest."

But it was too late. The study door flew open, the little red robe appeared on the threshold, joy put strength into the feeble limbs, and Beth ran straight into her father's arms. Never mind what happened just after that, for the full hearts overflowed, washing away the bitterness of the past and leaving only the sweetness of the present.

It was not at all romantic, but a hearty laugh set everybody straight again, for Hannah was discovered behind the door, sobbing over the fat Christmas turkey, which she had forgotten to put down when she rushed up from the kitchen. As the laugh subsided, Mrs. March began to thank Mr. Brooke for his faithful care of her husband, at which Mr. Brooke suddenly remembered that Mr. March needed rest, and seizing Laurie, he **precipitately retired**. Then the two invalids, Beth and Mr. March, were ordered to **repose**, which they did, by both sitting in one big chair and talking hard.

ESTIMABLE (<u>ess</u> ti muh buhl) *adj.*
worthy of respect
Synonyms: admirable, deserving

Mr. March told how he had longed to surprise them and how, when the fine weather came, he had been allowed by his doctor to take advantage of it, how devoted Brooke had been, and how Brooke was altogether a most **estimable** and upright young man. Why Mr. March paused a minute just there, and after a glance at Meg, who was violently poking the fire, looked at his wife with an inquiring lift of the eyebrows, I leave you to imagine. Also why Mrs. March gently nodded her head and asked, rather abruptly, if he wouldn't like to have something to eat. Jo saw and understood the look, and she stalked grimly away to get wine and beef tea, muttering to herself as she slammed the door, "I hate estimable young men with brown eyes!"

There never was such a Christmas dinner as they had that day. The fat turkey was a sight to behold, when Hannah sent it up, stuffed, browned, and decorated. So was the plum pudding, which melted in one's mouth, likewise the jellies, in which Amy reveled like a fly in a honeypot. Everything turned out well, which was a mercy, Hannah

FLUSTERED (<u>fluss</u> terd) *adj.*
anxious and upset
Synonyms: disturbed, chaotic

INFINITE (<u>in</u> fuh nit) *adj.*
without an end
Synonym: limitless

REMINISCE (rem uh <u>niss</u>) *v.* **-ing**, **-ed**
to talk or think about past events
Synonyms: recall, remember

DIGNITY (<u>dig</u> nuh tee) *n.*
a good sense of respect and pride
Synonyms: self-respect, poise

said, "For my mind was that **flustered** that it's a miracle I didn't roast the pudding and stuff the turkey with raisins, let alone <u>bilin'</u> of it in a cloth."

Mr. Laurence and his grandson dined with them, also Mr. Brooke, at whom Jo glowered darkly, to Laurie's **infinite** amusement. Two easy chairs stood side by side at the head of the table, in which sat Beth and her father, feasting modestly on chicken and a little fruit. They drank healths, told stories, sang songs, "**reminisced**," as the old folks say, and had a thoroughly good time. A sleigh ride had been planned, but the girls would not leave their father, so the guests departed early, and as twilight gathered, the happy family sat together round the fire.

"Just a year ago we were groaning over the dismal Christmas we expected to have. Do you remember?" asked Jo, breaking a short pause which had followed a long conversation about many things.

"Rather a pleasant year on the whole!" said Meg, smiling at the fire, and congratulating herself on having treated Mr. Brooke with **dignity**.

VALIANLTY (<u>val</u> yuhnt lee) *adv.*
done with courage and bravery
Synonyms: nobly, heroically

"I think it's been a pretty hard one," observed Amy, watching the light shine on her ring with thoughtful eyes.

"I'm glad it's over, because we've got you back," whispered Beth, who sat on her father's knee.

"Rather a rough road for you to travel, my little pilgrims, especially the latter part of it. But you have got on **valiantly**, and I think the burdens are in a fair way to tumble off very soon," said Mr. March, looking with fatherly satisfaction at the four young faces gathered round him.

"How do you know? Did Mother tell you?" asked Jo.

"Not much," replied her father. "Straws show which way the wind blows, and I've made several discoveries today."

"Oh, tell us what they are!" cried Meg, who sat beside him.

"Here is one." He pointed to the roughened forefinger, a burn on the back, and two or three little hard spots on the palm of Meg's hand. "I remember a time when this hand was white and smooth, and your first care was to keep it so. It

BLEMISH (<u>blem</u> ish) *n.*

an imperfection

Synonyms: mark, flaw

ACCOMPLISHMENT (uh <u>kom</u> plish muhnt) *n.*

1. great achievement or success
   Synonyms: triumph, feat
2. social grace, artistic talent
   Synonym: refinement

INDUSTRIOUS (in <u>duhss</u> tree uhss) *adj.*

hardworking and filled with energy

Synonyms: laborious, diligent

was very pretty then, but to me it is much prettier now, for in these seeming **blemishes** I read a little history. A burnt offering has been made to vanity, this hardened palm has earned something better than blisters, and I'm sure the sewing done by these pricked fingers will last a long time, so much good will went into the stitches. Meg, my dear, I value the womanly skill which keeps home happy more than white hands or fashionable **accomplishments**. I'm proud to shake this good, **industrious** little hand, and hope I shall not soon be asked to give it away."

If Meg had wanted a reward for hours of patient labor, she received it in the hearty pressure of her father's hand and the approving smile he gave her.

"In spite of the curly crop, I don't see the 'son Jo' whom I left a while ago," said Mr. March. "I see a young lady who pins her collar straight, laces her boots neatly, and neither whistles, talks slang, nor lies on the rug as she used to do. Her face is rather thin and pale just now, with watching and anxiety, but I like to look at it, for it has

FERAL (<u>fer</u> uhl) *adj.*
similar to a wild animal
Synonyms: untamed, undomesticated

grown gentler, and her voice is lower. She doesn't bounce, but moves quietly. I rather miss my **feral** girl, but if I get a strong, helpful, tenderhearted woman in her place, I shall feel quite satisfied. I don't know whether the trimming sobered our black sheep, but I do know that in all Washington I couldn't find anything beautiful enough to be bought with the five-and-twenty dollars my good girl sent me."

"Now, Beth," said Amy, longing for her turn, but ready to wait.

"She is not so shy as she used to be, and she has developed into such a strong, wonderful woman," began their father cheerfully.

Then he held her tightly and said, "I've got you safe and strong, my Beth, and I'll keep you so, please God."

After a minute's silence, he looked down at Amy, who sat at his feet, and said, with a caress of the shining hair, "I observed that Amy took drumsticks at dinner, ran errands for her mother all the afternoon, gave Meg her place tonight, and has waited on everyone with patience and good

CONCLUDE (kuhn <u>klood</u>) *v.* **-ing**, **-ed**
　to come to a decision or understanding
　　Synonyms: affirm, deduce

GRACEFUL (<u>grayss</u> fuhl) *adj.*
　displaying beauty and elegance
　　Synonyms: refined, stylish

CELEBRATE (<u>sel</u> uh brate) *v.* **-ing**, **-ed**
　to do something enjoyable at a special time
　　Synonym: rejoice

REUNION (ree <u>yoon</u> yuhn) *n.*
　a meeting between people after a long separation
　　Synonym: gathering

humor. I also observe that she does not fret much nor look in the glass, and she has not even mentioned a very pretty ring which she wears. So I **conclude** that she has learned to think of other people more and of herself less and that she has decided to try and mold her character as carefully as she molds her little clay figures. I am glad of this, for though I should be very proud of a **graceful** statue made by her, I shall be infinitely prouder of a lovable daughter with a talent for making life beautiful to herself and others. To all my girls, I love you so. Let us **celebrate** our **reunion** together for years to come."

SWARM (swarm) *v.* **-ing**, **-ed**
  to fly together in a group
    Synonyms: cluster, flock

ELDER (el dur) *adj.*
  born earlier than others
    Synonyms: older, senior

CHAPTER 12

Like bees **swarming** after their queen, mother and daughters hovered about Mr. March the next day, neglecting everything to look at, wait upon, and listen to the new invalid, who was in a fair way to be killed by kindness. As he sat propped up in a big chair by Beth's sofa, with the other three close by and Hannah popping in her head now and then "to peek at the dear man," nothing seemed needed to complete their happiness. But something was needed, and the **elder** ones felt it, though none confessed the fact.

SOBRIETY (soh <u>bry</u> uh tee) *n.*
a state of being without humor or wildness
Synonyms: seriousness, mirthlessness

MELODRAMATIC (mel uh druh <u>mat</u> ik) *adj.*
overemotional or sentimental
Synonyms: overly dramatic, exaggerated

IMPLORINGLY (im <u>plor</u> ing lee) *adv.*
pleadingly begging for something
Synonyms: beseechingly, entreatingly

BOON (boon) *n.*
something given
Synonyms: favor, gift

Mr. and Mrs. March looked at one another with an anxious expression, as their eyes followed Meg. Jo had sudden fits of **sobriety**, and was seen to shake her fist at Mr. Brooke's umbrella, which had been left in the hall. Meg was absent-minded, shy, and silent, started whenever the bell rang, and colored when John's name was mentioned. Amy said, "Everyone seemed waiting for something and couldn't settle down, which was queer, since Father was safe at home." And Beth innocently wondered why their neighbors didn't run over as usual.

Laurie went by in the afternoon, and seeing Meg at the window, seemed suddenly possessed with a **melodramatic** fit, for he fell down on one knee in the snow, beat his breast, tore his hair, and clasped his hands **imploringly**, as if begging some **boon**. And when Meg told him to behave himself and go away, he wrung imaginary tears out of his handkerchief, and staggered round the corner as if in utter despair.

"What does the goose mean?" said Meg, laughing and trying to look unconscious.

SCORNFULLY (<u>skorn</u> fehl ee) *adv.*
  done with contempt or anger
    Synonyms: mockingly, disdainfully

LINGER (<u>lin</u> gur) *v.* **-ing**, **-ed**
  to wait around or stay
    Synonyms: remain, loiter

PETTISHLY (<u>pet</u> ish lee) *adv.*
  done with an angry, sulky attitude
    Synonyms: irritably, testily

"He's showing you how your John will go on by-and-by. Touching, isn't it?" answered Jo **scornfully**.

"Don't say "my John." It isn't proper or true," but Meg's voice **lingered** over the words as if they sounded pleasant to her. "Please don't plague me, Jo, I've told you I don't care much about him, and there isn't to be anything said. But we are all to be friendly and go on as before."

"We can't, for something has been said, and Laurie's mischief has spoiled you for me. I see it, and so does Mother. You are not like your old self a bit and seem ever so far away from me. I don't mean to plague you and will bear it like a man, but I do wish it was all settled. I hate to wait, so if you mean ever to do it, make haste and have it over quickly," said Jo **pettishly**.

"I can't say anything till he speaks, and he won't, because Father said I was too young," began Meg, bending over her work with a queer little smile, which suggested that she did not quite agree with her father on that point.

"If he did speak, you wouldn't know what

DECISIVE (di <u>sy</u> siv) *adj.*
   able to make quick choices with ease, firm
      Synonyms: resolute, clear-thinking

FEEBLE (<u>fee</u> buhl) *adj.*
   not strong, very weak
      Synonyms: frail, delicate

TWILIGHT (<u>twy</u> lyt) *n.*
   time when the sun sets and it begins to get dark
      Synonyms: dusk, nightfall

to say but would cry or blush or let him have his own way, instead of giving a good, **decisive** no."

"I'm not so silly and **feeble** as you think. I know just what I should say, for I've planned it all, so I needn't be taken unawares. There's no knowing what may happen, and I wished to be prepared."

Jo couldn't help smiling at the important air which Meg had unconsciously assumed and which was as becoming as the pretty color in her cheeks.

"Would you mind telling me what you'd say?" asked Jo more respectfully.

"Not at all. You are sixteen now, quite old enough to be my <u>confidant</u>, and my experience will be useful to you by-and-by, perhaps, in your own affairs of this sort."

"Don't mean to have any. It's fun to watch other people be in love, but I should feel like a fool doing it myself," said Jo, looking alarmed at the thought.

"I think not, if you liked anyone very much, and he liked you." Meg spoke as if to herself, and glanced out at the lane where she had often seen lovers walking together in the summer **twilight**.

REVERIE (<u>rev</u> ur ee) *n.*
   a state of quiet thought
      Synonyms: daydream, contemplation

REHEARSE (ri <u>hurss</u>) *v.* **-ing**, **-ed**
   to prepare in advance
      Synonym: practice

ASPECT (<u>ass</u> pekt) *n.*
   the feature of something, a part
      Synonyms: appearance, look

"I thought you were going to tell your speech to that man," said Jo, rudely shortening her sister's little **reverie**.

"Oh, I should merely say, quite calmly and decidedly, 'Thank you, Mr. Brooke, you are very kind, but I agree with Father that I am too young to enter into any engagement at present, so please say no more, but let us be friends as we were.'"

"Hum, that's stiff and cool enough! I don't believe you'll ever say it, and I know he won't be satisfied if you do. If he goes on like the rejected lovers in books, you'll give in, rather than hurt his feelings."

"No, I won't. I shall tell him I've made up my mind, and I shall walk out of the room with dignity."

Meg rose as she spoke and was just going to **rehearse** the dignified exit, when a step in the hall made her fly into her seat and begin to sew as fast as if her life depended on finishing that particular seam in a given time. Jo smothered a laugh at the sudden change. And when someone gave a modest tap, she opened the door with a grim **aspect** which was anything but hospitable.

DIVULGING (di <u>vulj</u> ing) *adj.*
  showing or revealing something
    Synonym: telling

RETORT (ri <u>tort</u>) *n.*
  a sharp, quick reply
    Synonym: response

"Good afternoon. I came to get my umbrella, that is, to see how your father finds himself today," said Mr. Brooke, getting a trifle confused as his eyes went from one **divulging** face to the other.

"It's very well, he's in the rack. I'll get him, and tell it you are here." And having jumbled her father and the umbrella well together in her **retort**, Jo slipped out of the room to give Meg a chance to make her speech and air her dignity. But the instant she vanished, Meg began to sidle toward the door, murmuring, "Mother will like to see you. Pray sit down, I'll call her."

"Don't go. Are you afraid of me, Margaret?" Mr. Brooke looked so hurt that Meg thought she must have done something very rude. She blushed up to the little curls on her forehead, for he had never called her Margaret before, and she was surprised to find how natural and sweet it seemed to hear him say it. Anxious to appear friendly and at her ease, she put out her hand with a confiding gesture, and said gratefully, "How can I be afraid when you have been so kind to Father? I only wish I could thank you for it."

EXPEDITIOUSLY (eks puh <u>dish</u> uhss lee) *adv.*
done speedily and efficiently
Synonyms: quickly, swiftly

COMPASSIONATELY (kum <u>pash</u> uhn et lee) *adv.*
done with sympathy or with the desire to help
Synonyms: kindly, benevolently

REMUNERATION (ri myoon ur <u>ay</u> shun) *n.*
reward or pay exchanged for inconvenience
or work
Synonym: compensation

"Shall I tell you how?" asked Mr. Brooke, holding the small hand **expeditiously** in both his own, and looking down at Meg with so much love in the brown eyes that her heart began to flutter, and she both longed to run away and to stop and listen.

"Oh no, please don't, I'd rather not," she said, trying to withdraw her hand, and looking frightened in spite of her denial.

"I won't trouble you. I only want to know if you care for me a little, Meg. I love you so much, dear," added Mr. Brooke **compassionately**.

This was the moment for the calm, proper speech, but Meg didn't make it. She forgot every word of it, hung her head, and answered, "I don't know," so softly that John had to stoop down to catch the foolish little reply.

He seemed to think it was worth the trouble, for he smiled to himself as if quite satisfied, pressed the plump hand gratefully, and said in his most persuasive tone, "Will you try and find out? I want to know so much, for I can't go to work with any heart until I learn whether I am to have my **remuneration** in the end or not."

BESEECHING (bi <u>see</u> ching) *adj.*
pleading or begging for something
Synonyms: imploring, entreating

CAPRICIOUS (kuh <u>prish</u> uhss) *adj.*
unpredictable and tending to change one's mind
Synonyms: fickle, impulsive

"I'm too young," faltered Meg, wondering why she was so fluttered, yet rather enjoying it.

"I'll wait, and in the meantime you could be learning to like me. Would it be a very hard lesson, dear?"

"Not if I chose to learn it, but—"

"Please choose to learn, Meg. I love to teach, and this is easier than mathematics," broke in John, getting possession of the other hand, so that she had no way of hiding her face as he bent to look into it.

His tone was properly **beseeching**, but stealing a shy look at him, Meg saw that his eyes were merry as well as tender, and that he wore the satisfied smile of one who had no doubt of his success. This <u>nettled</u> her. She felt excited and strange, and not knowing what else to do, followed a **capricious** impulse, and, withdrawing her hands, said petulantly, "I don't choose. Please go away and let me be!"

"Do you really mean that?" he asked anxiously, following her as she walked away.

"Yes, I do. I don't want to be worried about

IMPISH (<u>imp</u> ish) *adj.*
  behaving in a troublesome, bad way
    Synonyms: naughty, mischievous

RELENT (ri <u>lent</u>) *v.* **-ing**, **-ed**
  to become more understanding or sympathetic
    Synonyms: concede, yield

such things. Father says I needn't, it's too soon and I'd rather not."

"Mayn't I hope you'll change your mind by-and-by? I'll wait and say nothing till you have had more time. Don't play with me, Meg. I didn't think that of you."

"Don't think of me at all. I'd rather you wouldn't," said Meg, taking an **impish** satisfaction in trying her lover's patience and her own power.

He was grave and pale now and looked decidedly more like the novel heroes whom she admired, but he neither slapped his forehead nor tramped about the room as they did. He just stood looking at her so longingly, so tenderly, that she found her heart **relenting** in spite of herself. What would have happened next I cannot say if Aunt March had not come hobbling in at this interesting minute.

The old lady couldn't resist her longing to see her nephew, for she had met Laurie as she took her airing, and hearing of Mr. March's arrival, drove straight out to see him. The family was all busy in the back part of the house, and she had

APPARITION (ap uh <u>rish</u> uhn) *n.*
something that looks like a ghost
Synonyms: phantom, specter

BLUNDER (<u>bluhn</u> dur) *v.* **-ing**, **-ed**
to make a foolish mistake
Synonym: bungle

SCANDALIZED (<u>skan</u> duh lyzd) *adj.*
shocked or outraged
Synonyms: appalled, outraged

made her way quietly in, hoping to surprise them. She did surprise two of them so much that Meg started as if she had seen an **apparition**, and Mr. Brooke vanished into the study.

"Bless me, what's all this?" cried the old lady with a rap of her cane as she glanced from the pale young gentleman to the blushing young lady.

"It's Father's friend. I'm so surprised to see you!" stammered Meg, feeling that she was in for a lecture now.

"That's evident," returned Aunt March, sitting down. "But what is Father's friend saying to make you look like a peony? There's mischief going on, and I insist upon knowing what it is," she said with another rap of her cane.

"We were only talking. Mr. Brooke came for his umbrella," began Meg, wishing that Mr. Brooke and the umbrella were safely out of the house.

"Brooke? That boy's tutor? I understand now. I know all about it. Jo **blundered** into a wrong message in one of your Father's letters, and I made her tell me. You haven't gone and accepted him, child?" cried Aunt March, looking **scandalized**.

DESTITUTE (<u>dess</u> tuh toot) *adj.*
　　lacking money, shelter, or food
　　　　Synonyms: poor, impoverished

PERVERSITY (pur <u>vurss</u> uh tee) *n.*
　　the condition of being unreasonable or
　　stubborn
　　　　Synonyms: irrationality, intransigence

PEREMPTORILY (pur <u>emp</u> tur uh lee) *adv.*
　　done with the expectation of obedience
　　　　Synonyms: authoritatively, dogmatically

RESOLUTE (rez uh <u>loot</u>) *adj.*
　　having made a firm decision
　　　　Synonym: determined

"Hush! He'll hear. Shan't I call Mother?" said Meg, much troubled.

"Not yet. I've something to say to you, and I must free my mind at once. Tell me, do you mean to marry this **destitute** man? If you do, not one penny of my money ever goes to you. Remember that, and be a sensible girl," said the old lady impressively.

Now Aunt March possessed in perfection the art of rousing the spirit of opposition in the gentlest people, and she enjoyed doing it. The best of us have a spice of **perversity** in us, especially when we are young and in love. If Aunt March had begged Meg to accept John Brooke, she would probably have declared she couldn't think of it, but as she was **peremptorily** ordered not to like him, she immediately made up her mind that she would. Inclination as well as perversity made the decision easy, and being already much excited, Meg opposed the old lady with unusual spirit.

"I shall marry whom I please, Aunt March, and you can leave your money to anyone you like," she said, nodding her head with a **resolute** air.

"Highty-tighty! Is that the way you take my

DILAPIDATED (duh <u>lap</u> uh day ted) *adj.*
in a state of decay, falling down
Synonyms: rundown, decrepit

INTERMISSION (in tur <u>mish</u> uhn) *n.*
a small break or rest in an event
Synonyms: interval, interlude

advice, Miss? You'll be sorry for it by-and-by, when you've tried love in a **dilapidated** hut and found it a failure."

"It can't be a worse one than some people find in big houses," retorted Meg.

Aunt March put on her glasses and took a look at the girl, for she did not know her in this new mood. Meg hardly knew herself, she felt so brave and independent, so glad to defend John and assert her right to love him, if she liked. Aunt March saw that she had begun wrong, and after a little **intermission**, made a fresh start, saying as mildly as she could, "Now, Meg, my dear, be reasonable and take my advice. I mean it kindly and don't want you to spoil your whole life by making a mistake at the beginning. You ought to marry well and help your family. It's your duty to make a rich match, and it ought to be impressed upon you."

"Father and Mother don't think so. They like John though he is poor."

"Your parents, my dear, have no more worldly wisdom than a pair of babies."

"I'm glad of it," cried Meg stoutly.

CROTCHETY (<u>kroch</u> uh tee) *adj.*
difficult to please, easily upset or made cross
Synonyms: grumpy, irritable

DECENT (<u>dee</u> sunt) *adj.*
respectable and kind
Synonyms: civilized, courteous

Aunt March took no notice but went on with her lecture. "This man is poor and hasn't got any rich relations, has he?"

"No, but he has many warm friends."

"You can't live on friends. Try it and see how cool they'll grow. He hasn't any business, has he?"

"Not yet. Mr. Laurence is going to help him."

"That won't last long. James Laurence is a **crotchety** old fellow and not to be depended on. So you intend to marry a man without money, position, or business, and to go on working harder than you do now, when you might be comfortable all your days by minding me and doing better? I thought you had more sense, Meg."

"I couldn't do better if I waited half my life! John is **decent** and wise, he's got heaps of talent, he's willing to work and sure to get on, he's so energetic and brave. Everyone likes and respects him, and I'm proud to think he cares for me, though I'm so poor and young and silly," said Meg, looking prettier than ever in her earnestness.

"He knows you have got rich relations, child. That's the secret of his liking, I suspect."

CALLOUSNESS (<u>kal</u> uhss nuhss) *n.*
a lack of concern for others' emotions
Synonyms: heartlessness, insensitivity

FICKLE (<u>fik</u> uhl) *adj.*
often changing one's mind
Synonyms: inconsistent, erratic

"Aunt March, how dare you say such a thing? John is above such **callousness**, and I won't listen to you a minute if you talk so," cried Meg indignantly, forgetting everything but the injustice of the old lady's suspicions. "My John wouldn't marry for money, any more than I would. We are willing to work, and we mean to wait. I'm not afraid of being poor, for I've been happy so far, and I know I shall be with him because he loves me, and I—"

Meg stopped there, remembering all of a sudden that she hadn't made up her mind, that she had told "her John" to go away, and that he might be overhearing her **fickle** remarks.

Aunt March was very angry, for she had set her heart on having her pretty niece make a fine match, and something in the girl's happy young face made the lonely old woman feel both sad and sour.

"Well, I wash my hands of the whole affair! You are a willful child, and you've lost more than you know by this piece of folly. No, I won't stop. I'm disappointed in you and haven't spirits to see your father now. Don't expect anything from me

DUDGEON (<u>duj</u> uhn) *n.*
    1. a state of indignation
      Synonym: outrage
    2. an angry tantrum or outburst
      Synonyms: fit, eruption

INHALATION (in huh <u>lay</u> shuhn) *n.*
    an inward breath
      Synonyms: gasp, gulp

ABUSE (uh <u>byooz</u>) *v.* **-ing**, **-ed**
    to treat in a harsh, cruel way
      Synonym: mistreat

when you are married. Your Mr. Brooke's friends must take care of you. I'm done with you forever."

Slamming the door in Meg's face, Aunt March drove off in high **dudgeon**. She seemed to take all the girl's courage with her, for when left alone, Meg stood for a moment, undecided whether to laugh or cry. Before she could make up her mind, she was taken possession of by Mr. Brooke, who said all in one **inhalation**, "I couldn't help hearing, Meg. Thank you for defending me and showing that you do care for me a little bit."

"I didn't know how much till she **abused** you," began Meg.

"And I needn't go away but may stay and be happy, may I, dear?"

Here was another fine chance to make the crushing speech and the stately exit, but Meg never thought of doing either, and disgraced herself forever in Jo's eyes by meekly whispering, "Yes, John," and hiding her face on Mr. Brooke's waistcoat.

Fifteen minutes after Aunt March's departure, Jo came softly downstairs, paused an instant at

TRANSFIXED (trans <u>fiksd</u>) *adj.*
held in place
Synonyms: frozen, fixed

OBJECTIONABLE (uhb <u>jek</u> shuh nuh buhl) *adj.*
unpleasant, given to offending people
Synonyms: obnoxious, irritating

SERENELY (suh <u>reen</u> lee) *adv.*
acting in a peaceful way
Synonyms: calmly, tranquilly

ENTHRONE (in <u>thrown</u>) *v.* **-ing, -ed**
to put on a throne or seat
Synonyms: place, install

ABJECT (<u>ahb</u> jekt) *adj.*
very humble or submissive
Synonyms: compliant, acquiescent

the parlor door, and hearing no sound within, nodded and smiled with a satisfied expression, saying to herself, "She has seen him away as we planned, and that affair is settled. I'll go and hear the fun, and have a good laugh over it."

But poor Jo never got her laugh, for she was **transfixed** upon the threshold by a sight which held her there, staring with her mouth nearly as wide open as her eyes. Going in to celebrate over a fallen enemy and to praise a strong-minded sister for the banishment of an **objectionable** lover, it certainly was a shock to behold the aforesaid enemy **serenely** sitting on the sofa, with the strong-minded sister **enthroned** upon his knee and wearing an expression of the most **abject** submission. Jo gave a sort of gasp, as if a cold shower bath had suddenly fallen upon her, for such an unexpected turning of the tables actually took her breath away. At the odd sound the lovers turned and saw her. Meg jumped up, looking both proud and shy, but "that man," as Jo called him, actually laughed and said coolly, as he kissed the astonished newcomer, "Sister Jo, congratulate us!"

TEMPESTUOUSLY (tem <u>pest</u> yoo us lee) *adv.*
   done in a violent way
      Synonyms: stormily, wildly

ELOQUENCE (<u>el</u> uh kwens) *n.*
   grace in speaking
      Synonyms: smoothness, loquaciousness

ASSEMBLE (uh <u>sem</u> buhl) *v.* **-ing**, **-ed**
   to bring together in a particular place
      Synonyms: gather, amass, construct

That was adding insult to injury. It was altogether too much, and making some wild demonstration with her hands, Jo vanished without a word. Rushing upstairs, she startled the invalids by exclaiming tragically as she burst into the room, "Oh, do somebody go down quick! John Brooke is acting dreadfully, and Meg likes it!"

Mr. and Mrs. March left the room with speed, and casting herself upon the bed, Jo cried and scolded **tempestuously** as she told the awful news to Beth and Amy. The little girls, however, considered it a most agreeable and interesting event, and Jo got little comfort from them, so she went up to her refuge in the garret, and confided her troubles to the rats.

Nobody ever knew what went on in the parlor that afternoon, but a great deal of talking was done, and quiet Mr. Brooke astonished his friends by the **eloquence** and spirit with which he pleaded his suit, told his plans, and persuaded them to **assemble** everything just as he wanted it.

The tea bell rang before he had finished describing the paradise which he meant to earn for

IMPECCABLY (im <u>pek</u> uh blee) *adv.*
perfectly or flawlessly, beyond criticism
Synonyms: faultlessly, spotlessly

ECSTATIC (ek <u>stat</u> ek) *adj.*
showing great pleasure or joy
Synonyms: delighted, elated

BLISSFUL (<u>bliss</u> ful) *adj.*
in a state of great happiness
Synonyms: happy, joyful

Meg, and he proudly took her in to supper, both of them looking so happy that Jo hadn't the heart to be jealous or sad. Amy was very much impressed by John's devotion and Meg's dignity, Beth beamed at them from a distance, while Mr. and Mrs. March surveyed the young couple with such tender satisfaction that it was **impeccably** evident Aunt March was right in calling them as "unworldly as a pair of babies." No one ate much, but everyone looked **ecstatic**, and the old room seemed to brighten up amazingly when the first romance of the family began there.

"You can't say nothing pleasant ever happens now, can you, Meg?" said Amy, trying to decide how she would group the lovers in a sketch she was planning to make.

"No, I'm sure I can't. How much has happened since I said that! It seems a year ago," answered Meg, who was in a **blissful** dream lifted far above such common things as bread and butter.

"The joys come close upon the sorrows this time, and I rather think the changes have begun," said Mrs. March. "In most families there

FEASIBLE (<u>fee</u> zuh buhl) *adj.*
capable of being accomplished
Synonyms: possible, achievable

GRAVITY (<u>grav</u> uh tee) *n.*
seriousness
Synonyms: importance, severity

comes, now and then, a year full of events. This has been such a one, but it ends well, after all."

"Hope the next will end better," muttered Jo, who found it very hard to see Meg absorbed in a stranger before her face, for Jo loved few persons very dearly and dreaded to have their affection lost or lessened in any way.

"I hope the third year from this will end better. I mean it shall, if I live to work out my plans," said Mr. Brooke, smiling at Meg, as if everything had become **feasible** to him now.

"Doesn't it seem very long to wait?" asked Amy, who was in a hurry for the wedding.

"I've got so much to learn before I shall be ready. It seems a short time to me," answered Meg, with a sweet **gravity** in her face never seen there before.

"You have only to wait, I am to do the work," said John beginning his labors by picking up Meg's napkin, with an expression which caused Jo to shake her head, and then say to herself with an air of relief as the front door banged, "Here comes Laurie. Now we shall have some sensible conversation."

DELUSION (di <u>loo</u> zhuhn) *n.*
a wrong idea or false impression
Synonyms: mirage, hallucination

APPRENTICE (uh <u>pren</u> tuhss) *n.*
one who studies with an experienced person
Synonyms: trainee, student

But Jo was mistaken, for Laurie came prancing in, overflowing with good spirits, bearing a great bridal-looking bouquet for "Mrs. John Brooke," and evidently laboring under the **delusion** that the whole affair had been brought about by his excellent management.

"I knew Brooke would have it all his own way, he always does, for when he makes up his mind to accomplish anything, it's done though the sky falls," said Laurie, when he had presented his offering and his congratulations.

"Much obliged for that recommendation. I take it as a good omen for the future and invite you to my wedding on the spot," answered Mr. Brooke, who felt at peace with all mankind, even his mischievous **apprentice**.

"I'll come if I'm at the ends of the earth, for the sight of Jo's face alone on that occasion would be worth a long journey. You don't look festive, ma'am, what's the matter?" asked Laurie, following her into a corner of the parlor, whither all had adjourned to greet Mr. Laurence.

"I don't approve of the match, but I've made up

my mind to bear it and shall not say a word against it," said Jo solemnly. "You can't know how hard it is for me to give up Meg," she continued with a little tremble in her voice.

"You don't give her up. You only go halves," said Laurie consolingly.

"It can never be the same again. I've lost my dearest friend," sighed Jo.

"You've got me, anyhow. I'm not good for much, I know, but I'll stand by you, Jo, all the days of my life. Upon my word I will!" And Laurie meant what he said.

"I know you will, and I'm ever so much obliged. You are always a great comfort to me, Laurie," returned Jo, gratefully shaking hands.

"Well, now, don't be dismal, there's a good fellow. It's all right you see. Meg is happy, Brooke will fly round and get settled immediately, Grandpa will attend to him, and it will be very jolly to see Meg in her own little house. We'll have capital times after she is gone, for I shall be through college before long, and then we'll go abroad on some nice trip or other. Wouldn't that console you?"

DECADE (<u>dek</u> ayd) *n.*
a period of ten years
Synonyms: span, era

PICTURESQUE (pik chur <u>esk</u>) *adj.*
pleasing to the eyes, well-formed
Synonyms: striking, beautiful

"I rather think it would, but there's no knowing what may happen in three years," said Jo thoughtfully.

"That's true. Don't you wish you could take a look forward and see where we shall all be then? I do," returned Laurie.

"I think not, for I might see something sad, and everyone looks so happy now, I don't believe they could be much improved." And Jo's eyes went slowly round the room, brightening as they looked, for the prospect was a pleasant one.

Father and Mother sat together, quietly reliving the first chapter of the romance, which for them began two **decades** ago. Amy was drawing the lovers, who sat apart in a **picturesque** world of their own, the light of which touched their faces with a grace the little artist could not copy. Beth lay on her sofa, talking cheerily with her old friend, Mr. Laurence, who held her little hand as if he felt that it possessed the power to lead him along the peaceful way she walked. Jo lounged in her favorite low seat, with the grave quiet look which best became her, and Laurie, leaning on

RECEPTION (ri <u>sep</u> shun) *n.*
response given to something new
Synonym: welcome

the back of her chair, his chin on a level with her curly head, smiled with his friendliest aspect, and nodded at her in the long glass which reflected them both.

So the curtain falls upon Meg, Jo, Beth, and Amy. Whether it ever rises again, depends upon the **reception** given the first act of the domestic drama called *Little Women*.

RESOURCES

GLOSSARY

The following are words and terms that you are not likely to be tested on, but understanding them may enhance your appreciation of the text.

air (ayr) *n.*
1. the appearance of something
2. artificial behavior, pretense
3. a song

arnica (<u>ar</u> nih kah) *n.*
a mixture of herbs often used in healing injuries

bilin' (by lin) *v.* **-ing**, **-ed**
Hannah's mispronunciation of *boil,* meaning "to cook in water"

blancmange (blahnk <u>mahnj</u>) *n.*
a sweet desert made from milk and gelatin

bookworm (<u>buk</u> wurm) *n.*
an informal term for someone who loves books

breeding (<u>breed</u> ing) *n.*
upbringing

confidant (<u>kon</u> fuh dahnt) *n.*
a person to whom one gives private information

Christopher Columbus *person*
Italian-born explorer (1451–1506), in this case
used as an exclamation

colt (kohlt) *n.*
a young horse

conservatory (kon <u>suhrv</u> ah toree) *n.*
an inside space for growing and displaying
plants

fighting (<u>fyt</u> ing) *n.*
battle or combat, in this case, the American
Civil War (1861–1865)

geranium (jeh <u>ray</u> nee uhm) *n.*
a plant; with white, pink, or red flowers

harum-scarum (<u>hare</u> uhm <u>scare</u> uhm) *adj.*
reckless

hose (hoze) *n.*
informal term for hosiery, meaning socks or
stockings

label (<u>lay</u> buhl) *n.*
Amy March's mispronunciation of *libel,*
meaning "to slander"

lullaby (<u>luhl</u> uh by) *n.*
a song sung to get a child to fall asleep

mantelpiece (<u>man</u> tel pees) *n.*
a wood, stone, or brick structure around a
fireplace

Marmee (<u>mar</u> mee) *n.*
the March sisters' pet name for their mother,
probably coming from a childish pronunciation
of *Mommy*

nettle (<u>net</u> tuhl) *v.* **-ing**, **-ed**

to annoy or anger

Pilgrim's Progress *n.*

First published in 1678, John Bunyan's work was, on one level, the story of a simple individual's journey from his home city, which he believes is about to be destroyed. On another level it was the tale of a soul trying to make the journey to Heaven. *Pilgrim's Progress* was popular for centuries, and many people treated it as a guidebook for how to live a good, moral life and how to deal with the many difficulties a moral person faced in this world.

poplin (<u>pop</u> lin) *n.*

a tightly woven cotton cloth

pops (popz) *n.*

an informal term for clothes made of poplin

trump (truhmp) *n.*

an old-fashioned term for "a helpful person"

sect (sekt) *n.*
    Amy March's mispronunciation of *sex,*
    meaning "gender"

snow maiden *n.*
    a young woman with such light-colored hair
    and skin that she seems to resemble snow

telegraph (<u>tel</u> uh graf) *n.*
    a system for transmitting messages along a
    wire; during the middle of the 19th century,
    the telegraph was a new and exciting means of
    communication.

without (wi <u>thowt</u>) *adv.*
    outside

WRITING A BOOK REPORT
ABOUT *LITTLE WOMEN*

The key to writing a good report is to organize your ideas before you start writing. Use the following questions to organize your ideas for a book report about *Little Women*.

1. What is the title?
2. Who is the author? What do you know about the author and her life?
3. When and where does the story take place?
4. Who are the main characters of the book?
5. What happens to these people during the story? What are these people like at the beginning? And at the end? What problems do these people face? How do these people solve those problems?
6. What does the book tell you about life at the time the novel takes place?
7. What do you think is the main theme or idea of the book?
8. What is the main thing you learned from this book?
9. What would you tell a friend about this book if he or she asked you about it?

DISCUSSION QUESTIONS
ABOUT *LITTLE WOMEN*

Here are several questions to think about and to discuss with classmates, friends, and other people who have read Louisa May Alcott's *Little Women*:

1. In what ways is the title *Little Women* a fitting title for the book? Why or why not?

2. The author is careful to describe each of the March sisters – her looks, her personality, and even her talents and goals – in detail. In what ways are the sisters alike? In what ways are they different?

3. Does the author seem to be more sympathetic to, or to "like," any one of the March sisters more than the others? What makes you think this?

4. For many readers, Jo is an important figure. What is it about her that would make her so interesting – and even admirable – to these readers?

5. The March sisters seem particularly talented at making friends: people who like them, appreciate them, and who are even willing to help them in times of difficulty. What are some of the more memorable examples of this that take place within the book?

6. Today, many books and films are "re-tellings" of classic tales. Suppose you were given the task of revising *Little Women* and giving it a modern setting. What would you change about it? How would it be different from and the same as the book you have just read?

7. Little Women is very much a story of how family members relate to one another. Do you think it is an accurate, realistic portrait of this? Or is it an idealized version of a family?

8. What do you think will happen to each of the March sisters in the few years that follow the ending of this book?